Christmas on the Bay

A Collection of Holiday Stories
from the
Chesapeake Bay Writers

For information contact :
Blue Fortune Enterprises, LLC
Lavender Press
P.O. Box 554
Yorktown, VA 23690
http://blue-fortune.com

ISBN: 978-1-961548-16-9

First Edition: September 2024

To all the storytellers:
Stories nurture the world, and they tell us where we've been
while shining a light on where we're going.
Thank you for sharing your words.

Table of Contents

Dear Reader,

In 2009, I was a new writer looking for guidance, information and inspiration. I did some research about area critique groups and found a home with the fabulous Richard and Emmeline Bailey in Williamsburg, Virginia. They opened their home to host writers every month, providing a place where we could talk, share, laugh, and ask questions. They were also, I soon learned, an integral part of a group called Chesapeake Bay Writers (CBW).

I joined CBW and soon after joined the board of directors as well. Although it has been a few years since I was a part of the board, there is a special place in my heart for this merry band of wordsmiths who support and encourage each other in all things writing.

CBW supports writers in all stages of their writing journey, from the nuts and bolts of putting together a manuscript, to editing, to publication, and everything in between. The objectives of the CBW are to further the craft of writing; to provide members with opportunities for connecting and exchanging ideas with others who share similar interests; to assist and encourage members in their efforts to achieve their writing-related goals; and to offer educational and informative programs about writing and marketing finished works.

If you are a writer and looking for a home, I suggest you reach out to your local writers' group. If you cannot find one, send us an email. We would be happy to help.

In 2013, I worked with the fabulous writer/publisher Greg Lilly on the first CBW anthology, *Harboring Secrets*. Although he has since moved to another part of Virginia, I contacted Greg to ask about that anthology. He gave me all the information I needed, and when I approached the current CBW board, we were ready for a new project.

We hope you enjoy this collection of holiday short stories from members of the Chesapeake Bay Writers.

Happy holidays,

Narielle Living
Publisher

A Corduroy Christmas

by Patti Gaustad Procopi

"Christmas? Have you really thought about this? You know what Mom is like at Christmas."

My sister laughed. "It will be marvelous. What better time to introduce someone to the family? Christmas is a time of love and warmth and happiness."

I rolled my eyes, which thankfully Lexi couldn't see over the phone. "They say Christmas is actually full of stress and unhappiness and despair. I've read suicides go up drastically over the holidays."

"If people have your attitude about the holidays, that's probably true. Thankfully, most of us are full of the joy of the season. Now, your mission is to get Tony ready for the trip. Make sure he gets a suit. I'm counting on you, Izzie. Don't let me down." My sister hung up.

I collapsed on my bed. How did my sister always manage to inveigle me in her plans and plots? Try as I might, I couldn't resist her.

She was such a Pollyanna, always seeing the best in people and events. Despite all evidence to the contrary, she still believed Christmas at our house was a wonderful family affair.

It wasn't. My mother treated Christmas as something akin to the D-Day invasion. Every detail, every moment, was planned out to the Nth degree. Each day had a schedule we adhered to with military precision. Each year Christmas had a different theme, and all the adornments and trimmings must relate.

Planning for next year started as soon as the decorations were packed, labeled, and stored away. Mother kept a file so she could reuse things if they fit the new theme.

This year's theme was *The Wizard of Oz*. For the life of me, I couldn't figure out what it had to do with Christmas. What about Jesus? Angels? Shepherds? Wisemen? I'd even prefer Santa and the reindeer. But the effing Wizard of Oz?

The best fifteen-foot-tall artificial tree would be decorated from top to bottom by a team of young men who could climb up and down ladders without plummeting to their deaths. Mother stood below, watching their work, suggesting ornament placements to ensure no spots were left bare.

In keeping with the theme, the tree and house were decorated in ruby red and emerald green. The red ornaments were recycled from the *Gone with the Wind* Christmas of five years earlier. They were called 'Scarlet' red that year. "Waste not, want not," Mother said, proudly announcing she'd be able to use some of the red ornaments. Ten years of Christmas decorations packed in totes took up half the basement, and she thought she should be congratulated for re-using some red stuff.

A *Gone with the Wind* Christmas? Sigh. I remembered that one. Once again, what did it have to do with Christmas? When Lexi and I were little, Christmas was normal with normal decorations. The tree was covered with handmade ornaments, candy canes, and strings of popcorn. Then we moved into a huge house in a gated community and mother learned Christmas in First Landing Estates was not a celebration but a competition. A competition she was determined to win.

And now, Lexi wanted to bring an outsider into this madness. Into this carefully orchestrated, not very merry, family Christmas.

Lexi fancied herself an avant-garde artist and decided to attend college in New York. Virginia was much too provincial for her. There she met Tony. He was one of her professors. It was, according to her, love at first sight. They hung out in artsy student-teacher groups, smoking and drinking cheap wine.

I decided to go to the same school because I missed Lexi. However, as soon as I arrived at the start of Lexi's junior year, she left. She and Tony had a fight and Lexi fled home, to the boring but familiar environs of Williamsburg.

Tony did not give up easily. Many phone calls were made. Many tears were shed. And Lexi hatched a plan for Tony to come for the holidays.

I liked Tony. However, I didn't think Mom and Dad (especially Mom) would. He was a typical 1970's art professor. Scruffy. Hairy. Smoked (various things) and drank. And he was poor. But his biggest fault was he was Italian. Which, to my mother, the ultimate WASP, meant he wasn't an Anglo-Saxon or a Protestant. Tony's family was probably Catholic, which my mother thought was akin to being a member of a cult. And to top it off, he was a Yankee. And Lexi wanted to introduce him to the family during the height of the most stressful time of the year?

Tony asked me to go suit shopping with him. And despite my misgivings with the plan, I agreed. Tony showed up in his ancient Volvo station wagon—the standard college professor vehicle, though his had seen some rough years. It coughed and sputtered, belching black smoke. Sitting in the passenger seat, I noticed daylight coming through the floorboards. I thought of my father's Buick

LeSabre and winced.

Assuming we'd be going to a fancy department store, I was surprised when Tony drove to a strip mall and parked in front of "Honest Frankie's Discount Suit Shop." There was a garish sign on the window - "Ya gonna love how you look." I couldn't imagine my father shopping at such a place.

Tony must have seen my expression as he opened the door. "This place comes highly recommended."

By who?

"I wanted to be sure to get something nice. Lexi says your mother is a bit persnickety."

A bit?

Tony told the clerk he needed a good suit because he was meeting his girlfriend's parents over the holidays. He leaned closer and whispered. I caught the word "price" and "not more than…"

"We got just the thing," the salesman nodded. "The latest fashion and a real bargain to boot."

"I need something ready to go." Tony said, as he took off his oversized jacket.

"I got it. I understand," the salesmen said as he measured Tony's arms, legs, and shoulders. "Trust me."

Stripped down to his boxers and t-shirt, I noticed how oddly shaped Tony was. His legs were short and bowed out. His chest was large, but his arms were long and thin. It was not going to be easy to get a suit off the rack without some adjustments.

The salesmen pointed to a fitting room. "Wait there. I gotta couple in your size. Yah gonna love 'em."

He brought Tony two suits and walked over to me. "So, you the girlfriend?" He grinned. He had a gold tooth. And a pinky ring. This was like a bad movie.

"No. That would be my sister. She's back home. I'm here helping out." Why, oh why, oh why, did I get involved? The knot in my stomach hardened. A sense of impending doom enveloped me.

Tony stepped out in a dark brown wide-wale corduroy suit. With his shaggy black hair, long sideburns, dark skin and huge tinted glasses, he looked horrible. Like a shaggy dog standing on its hind legs. I stifled a gasp.

"What do you think?" Tony asked, looking in the mirror. I thought corduroy was not a good choice for him. Possibly for anyone. When did they start making corduroy suits? This suit was ill fitting and ill conceived.

"Does it come in another color?" I asked. Another color might be better. It couldn't be worse.

"Yeah. A nice light brown. I put that one in the fitting room, too." The salesman smiled yanking on the sleeves and legs. "This one fits ya great."

We obviously had a different opinion of fits great.

A moment later, Tony emerged in the identical suit in a different color. Was this better? The lighter color was possibly an improvement, though it was an odd shade of brown. "Let's get a shirt and tie to perk this up," I suggested.

"Good idea," said the salesman. Together we picked a shirt and a tie, which hopefully pulled it all together. Not great but not bad. Tony smiled at himself in the mirror.

When the salesman rang him up, I saw Tony wince. It seemed quite cheap for a suit, but Tony had to pay for his plane ticket and money was probably tight.

I got home to Williamsburg a few days before Tony was due to arrive. All was calm. All was bright. The house looked amazing. The *Wizard of Oz* tree glistened in ruby red and emerald green. Actually, the entire house glittered in red and green splendor.

"I know I will win in several categories this year," my mother announced gleefully. "Take that, Pookie Smyth-Jones. You are about to be dethroned. There's a new Christmas Queen."

"Hi Mom," I said, hauling my suitcase up the stairs. "So nice to be home. The house looks great."

She leaned over to give me a quick hug. "Lovely to have you home, dear. It's what the holidays are all about. Family."

Really Mom? Seems it's all about winning.

Lexi came bounding in to my room. "I can't believe Tony will be here soon. This is going to be the best

Christmas ever! I know Mom and Dad will love him."

"I'm sure you're right. What's not to love? He's a poor, scruffy college professor, not to mention too old for you, Italian and Catholic."

Lexi laughed. "You're so funny."

Amazing. How did she manage to completely ignore reality?

"Now, I have to know. He's all set for the holidays? All the right clothes? All the right…". She paused as if she couldn't quite finish the thought. Right what? Right pedigree? Right family? Right religion? The answer was no to all of the above.

"Yes, he's all set. He bought a suit. I suggested what clothes he'd need to bring. Casual but elegant." I was putting my clothes away while I spoke.

"He has casual elegant clothes?" Lexi was mystified.

"No, he doesn't!" I spun around, "And you knew that before you came up with this hare-brained scheme. I told him to bring his 'best' clothes. Hopefully he has something with no rips, patches, or paint stains."

"At least he has a suit. He can dress it up or down. Dad can loan him a few things."

I blanched, thinking of the wide-wale, light-brown corduroy suit. "Hopefully," I squeaked. "Maybe a sweater might fit? A cardigan? A vest?"

"Dad does have some lovely cashmere sweaters." Lexi said, dancing out of the room with stars in her eyes.

There's an old expression about even if you put lipstick on a pig, it will still be a pig... or wait... you can't make a silk purse from a pig's ear? I doubted Tony's appearance could be enhanced, even sporting one of Dad's cashmere sweaters.

I was overcome by despair. I knew how much this meant to Lexi. She pictured a perfect family Christmas. The first of many. She envisioned us all waking up Christmas morning in our matching plaid pajamas and eating pancakes with fresh cream. Afterwards, we'd gather around the red and green bejeweled tree and exchange gifts. It simply wasn't going to happen. No matter how hard she wished, dreamed, and hoped.

Tony no doubt loved Lexi and wanted to make her happy. What he didn't understand was Lexi was used to the finer things in life. Even though she might enjoy playing at being a bohemian artist at college, she was destined to live her life in the suburbs, attending teas, PTA meetings and playing tennis at the country club.

That was not the immediate issue. We needed to get through the visit. I counted up the days and events he'd have to survive. It was like some ancient game of endurance.

The first day he'd arrive late in the evening. There'd only be time for introductions and a snack. A check mark for easy and survivable.

On the second day we'd have to make ourselves scarce

since the judges would be making their rounds. Out of sight. Out of mind. Another easy check.

Christmas Eve would be the biggest challenge and the potential for disaster was high. Brunch at the country club was the social event of the season. This is where the corduroy suit would make its debut. That evening was the second major event of the holidays—midnight mass at church, followed by a champagne reception. Tony only had one suit, so he'd have to wear it again. Not good. Maybe we could borrow a tie from Dad to freshen the look? Day Three had many landmines, though maybe I was worrying unnecessarily and Tony and the suit would sail through the day triumphantly.

Christmas was a simple family day with breakfast and gifts. No need for a suit. Would there be any presents for Tony? Would Tony have any presents for the family? Not worth worrying about. Possibly awkward, but survivable.

The day after Christmas is known as Judgement Day in First Landing. Mom hosted a big open house for her friends, neighbors, and competitors. Afterwards, we'd all head to the park to hear the winners announced. A suit was not required at the open house, so we could put that dog to rest. Another easy day.

The sixth day was the end of the visit. Nothing to do except pack and say goodbye before driving back to the airport. Depending on whether she'd won or lost, Mother might not even notice Tony's departure.

Overall, the visit was survivable with only a few minor wounds.

D-Day finally arrived. Hopefully not Doomsday. Lexi and I drove Dad's Buick to the Richmond airport to pick up Tony. I waited in the car while Lexi went to meet him at the gate. I wanted to give them a few moments of privacy.

They showed up holding hands and gazing lovingly into each other's eyes. Whatever caused their initial breakup was a thing of the past. Tony threw his suitcase in the trunk and climbed in the back with Lexi. Obviously, I was the chauffeur. "Hey Izzy," he said. "Wow, nice car. Looks brand new."

"It is," Lexi said. "My dad gets a new car every other year and my mom gets the old one." Tony looked around in awe. I thought of his ancient rattle trap Volvo.

When we arrived, Lexi led Tony to the door by his hand. He'd been staring incredulously at the neighborhood decorations as we drove along. Lexi explained about the competition and how obsessed Mother was with winning. He'd been speechless as we drove along. Now he stared down at "The Yellow Brick Road" Mother created on the path to our front door.

We walked in and Mom called out, "We're in the den."

Tony stared at the fifteen-foot tall emerald and ruby tree in the foyer. "Wow." He muttered.

Lexi said, "Time to meet Mom and Dad."

"Sure. Okay." Tony was babbling as he wiped his hands on his pants. I noticed his jeans were not torn, stained, or rumpled. A good sign. Dad stood up and put his hand out. "So, this is the famous Tony," he said with a smile. Tony smiled back, shaking Dad's hand. Mom stood up and everyone was talking at once. I sat on a chair in the corner, watching.

After some refreshments and cordial conversation, Lexi suggested Tony was probably tired. She said she'd show him to his room. Mom and Dad said goodnight and sat back down in their chairs. I followed Lexi and Tony. He was staying in the basement guestroom which was quite nice. Originally, Mom's parents planned to move in, so we fixed the room up. Then they decided to move to Florida instead. It was cozy with a little fireplace, though I don't remember it ever being used.

At the top of the stairs, Tony was snuggling Lexi, telling her how much he'd missed her. "Come down later for a real welcome." She demurred, saying Mom was a light sleeper and she didn't want to be caught. Tony was understandably upset by this turn of events. He must have assumed they'd be staying in the same room. "We're all adults here," he said.

"Yes, we are, but unmarried adults," she replied, kissing him softly and brushing his hair out of his eyes. "See you in the morning."

I followed Lexi back up to her room. She gave me a

huge grin. "It's going great. Just like I thought."

"Early days," I replied. "It's not like Mom and Dad are going to be rude to a guest in their home."

"True. Still, I'm pleased with how things are going."

It had only been three hours. Day One got a checkmark.

At breakfast Mom was already in a dither. Best to leave as soon as possible and stay gone until dinner time. One never knew when the judges might arrive. Lexi borrowed Mom's car, announcing she was going to show Tony the sights and have lunch in town. Dad retreated to his office and shut the door. I was abandoned. It was time to check out the competition, so I headed out into the neighborhood.

We all returned to the house at 5:00 pm, which was the official time the judging ended. Mother looked exhausted. It was always hard to read the judge's reaction. I told her after checking out the other houses, I was confident this one was in the bag. She smiled weakly. Dinner was quiet. Tony and Lexi looked ecstatic. They couldn't keep their eyes off each other and kept playing footsie under the table. So childish. Day Two checked off with no disasters. So far so good.

Christmas Eve dawned bright. After coffee, we all retreated to our rooms to get ready for brunch. Mother always took an inordinate amount of time dressing. Lexi and I were ready first and waited for Tony to join us. I took several deep breaths, hoping the corduroy suit looked better than I remembered.

Tony walked up the stairs, and Lexi gasped. He smiled up at her. The suit looked awful. It was worse than I remembered. In the bright light of day, the suit wasn't light-brown, more yellow, like the color of baby diarrhea.

Lexi dug her nails into my wrist and muttered, "Come with me," while smiling at Tony. "I'll be back in a sec. Wait in the den. Izzy and I have some last-minute things to take care of."

She dragged me through the kitchen and out into the garage. "I asked you to do one thing! One thing!" She was trying not to yell, so her voice came out in strangled yips. "Help Tony pick out a nice suit, and this is what you helped him pick? This corduroy monstrosity the color of vomit?" Her eyes filled with tears. I felt terrible.

"Lexi. I'm sorry. I told you I wasn't any good at this. We went to some awful discount men's store, and he told the clerk how much he had to spend, and this is what they had in his price range."

"It didn't come in any other color?" she wailed.

"Yes, it did. But trust me, the other color was even worse. It was dark brown, and it made him look swarthy, like a pirate. This one was better with his coloring."

"This isn't better with anyone's coloring!" She was on the verge of hysteria. "Why didn't you loan him some money or something or anything? This is going to be a disaster. Can you imagine Mother walking into the country club with Tony in this suit?"

"You know Tony doesn't have much money. After paying for his plane ticket, he didn't have much left for a suit. I told you this was a bad idea. Christmas was the worst time to meet the family."

The door opened and Dad appeared, looking quizzically at both of us. "What are you two doing in the garage? Tony is waiting in the den and your mom will be down in a minute."

"Just some Christmas plotting," I said, trying to look mischievous. "You know Christmas! So many surprises."

Dad laughed. Thankfully, he's not the suspicious type. Mother would have grilled us until we broke down and confessed everything.

We walked into the den. Tony stood awkwardly. Had he picked up on Lexi's horror over his suit? "Hope you're hungry," Dad said. "The brunch at the club is a killer." He stopped, looking more closely at Tony's suit. You could tell he was confused. He didn't know much about fashion. His tailor advised him on what he should wear.

"Corduroy," Dad mused. "Is that coming back into fashion? I remember wearing corduroy as a kid. You don't see it much anymore." He paused before adding, "Interesting color."

"The man at the suit store said it was the newest thing," Tony replied. I think it began to dawn on him he might have been conned. He yanked nervously on the cuffs and hem of the jacket.

Mother walked in and almost recoiled. The look on her face was enough to make the rest of us recoil. She struggled for a moment before composing herself. "Are we all ready?" Her voice was unnaturally high. "Time to go."

Mother sailed through the club, barely acknowledging the greetings of friends. She obviously didn't want to introduce Tony. She merely waved, staring straight ahead as we trailed behind.

Never had a more miserable bunch graced the Christmas Eve brunch. Mother was mortified. Father was confused. Lexi was furious at me. I was furious at Lexi. And Tony was devastated. His moment of glory. His moment to shine in front of Lexi's family had all been undone by the unfortunate choice of a diarrhea-colored, wide-wale corduroy suit.

When we returned home, Tony ran down the stairs to his room. Lexi gave me one last dirty look before running up to her room. I slumped down on the couch. How had this become all my fault?

We reassembled in the living room around six to get a quick bite before church. Everyone claimed to still be full from brunch, even though we'd hardly eaten anything.

Mother arrived with a sweater and a necktie of Dad's which she handed to Tony. "Lexi told me you inadvertently left some of your clothes behind. Hopefully this will fit."

I glanced at Tony. Now he knew his suit choice had been the worst decision ever. Lexi was ashamed of him. He mutely took the sweater and tie and went back downstairs to change. When he came back, he didn't look at any of us.

The sweater fit. Not perfectly, still, it fit, and Dad's expensive silk tie enhanced the outfit. Tony wore the corduroy pants since the only other pants he'd brought he was saving for the Judgement Day brunch. I noticed how the corduroy pants accentuated Tony's short, bowed legs.

We walked silently to church. It was a gorgeous star filled night and I hoped and prayed this was the last bad moment of the trip. Day Three had not been a great success, still we'd survived by the skin of our teeth.

The service was lovely. The music amazing, as always. Even Tony appeared to relax. Lexi took his hand and he didn't pull his hand away. At the reception, Lexi followed Mom and Dad, introducing Tony. Reluctantly he allowed Lexi to drag him around, appearing to deflate with each step.

Christmas day dawned with bright sunshine and crisp, cold air. We all slowly made our way to the kitchen where Dad fried up enough bacon to clog all our arteries, followed by stacks and stacks of pancakes until we begged him to stop.

Taking our coffee, we went to sit around the tree. It was a beautiful tree and if it hadn't been given the title of *The Wizard of Oz* tree, I'd have liked it.

Dad played the role of Santa, pulling out presents to hand to everyone. There were gifts for Tony and he brought gifts for everyone. He presented my parents a portrait of Lexi in wild, psychedelic colors. They expressed great admiration for his artistic efforts. I couldn't see it fitting in with their décor. I also got a small print. He gave Lexi a beautiful necklace an artist friend made. She claimed to love it, but I sensed a distinct chill in the air.

After clearing up, the men retreated to the den to watch TV and the women went to the kitchen to start Christmas dinner. This was a meal to rival Thanksgiving. We cooked for hours before finally gathering to enjoy the feast. Or pretending to enjoy the feast. An odd mood settled over our gathering. I knew Mother was tense because tomorrow was Judgement Day; however, I couldn't determine what was going on with Tony and Lexi. I thought things had improved. Immediately after dinner, Lexi announced she had a headache and went to bed. Still we survived Day Four.

Judgement Day dawned bright, another one of those picture-perfect Virginia winter days. We all got our own breakfast because Mother was busy getting ready for the caterers and making sure all the decorations inside and out were perfect.

For today's events, Tony wore a pair of khaki pants with another one of Dad's sweaters. He looked miserable. He and Lexi were ignoring each other. The caterers arrived and set out tons of food. I wasn't hungry but started nervously snacking. People arrived and gushed over Mother's decorations. The "Yellow Brick Road" drew rave reviews.

At 5:00, everyone in the neighborhood went to the park to await the big moment. The judges huddled in front of a microphone. Finally one stepped forward to read the list of winners. It was a total coup for Mother. She won best-in-show (or whatever they called it) and several other categories, including one for the "Yellow Brick Road". Everyone clapped. Hugs and handshakes were exchanged among winners and losers. Mother and Pookie embraced and gave each other fake kisses on the cheeks. On the surface it was all quite congenial with an undercurrent of hurt and resentment.

Finally, the judges announced the theme for next year's competition was *Scheherazade and the 1,0001 Nights*. I could almost hear the gears in Mom's head start spinning. She whispered in my ear. "I can reuse the gold coins from *Treasure Island*." I almost said, "How about next year we do Jesus?"

Day five was over and tomorrow Tony was flying home. Overall, it went quite well. The only off note was the corduroy suit. Though honestly, I couldn't figure out why everyone got so worked up about it. Sure, the suit was cheap and ugly, but it was hardly the end of the world. No one died.

I woke to angry voices from the living room. I got up

and crept to the top of the stairs. It sounded like Tony and Lexi were bickering.

I slipped down the stairs to listen. Peeking into the living room I saw them standing stiffly, gesturing angrily. They were arguing about the damn suit. And of course, I was being blamed again. The only thing they appeared to agree on was I planned to embarrass Tony by getting him to buy that damn suit! I wanted to run into the room and slap them both. Tony was also going on about how pretentious we were and my Mother could feed a third-world country with all the money she wasted on Christmas decorations.

Lexi got her share of blame. She was a spoiled rich girl, who enjoyed hanging out with her working-class boyfriend to show off how open-minded she was, while secretly sneering at him. And it went on and on. Finally, she shouted she couldn't wait until tomorrow, and he stormed back downstairs saying it would be the happiest day of the trip.

I ran up to my room before Lexi caught me spying. I seethed with anger at them entangling me in their pathetic relationship. I didn't want to get involved in the first place.

The *beep beep beep* of the fire alarm woke me. I jumped out of bed, fearing the house was on fire. Mom and Dad and Lexi were in the hallway.

My father shepherded us down the steps. "I've called the fire department. We need to get outside."

"What about Tony?" Lexi shouted hysterically.

"I'll get Tony," Father replied, heading down to the basement.

Firetrucks wailed in the distance as we waited on the sidewalk. Dad came out alone. "I couldn't get into the basement. It's filled with smoke. I called his name. He couldn't have slept through the alarm. He probably went out the back door."

Lexi buried her head into Mom's shoulder. Mother looked stricken. For a moment I honestly thought she was concerned about Tony until I heard her moan, "My totes. My decorations. All gone."

The firemen were quickly on the scene. Lexi shouted at them to look for Tony. Fifteen minutes later the chief came out and walked up to us. "You're lucky. Not really a fire, just a lot of smoke. We found something smoldering in the basement fireplace." He held up a scrap of cloth. Through the soot we could see a bit of light brown wide-wale corduroy.

"Must have been an accident," the chief said. "It appears the flue wasn't open. Maybe your guest wasn't familiar with fireplaces?"

Tony and his suitcase were gone. Mom was relieved to discover her totes of decorations survived. Dad was happy the house hadn't burned down. Lexi was not speaking to me.

It was a deliberate message. "Take that you snobs," he

probably said as he shoved his suit in the fireplace before grinding his cigarette into the fabric to set it on fire. It made me sad. He'd been so proud of that suit. And looked forward to meeting the family.

I planned on enrolling in the local college next semester.

Patti Gaustad Procopi is a former army brat who lived all over the world before settling in Gloucester, Virginia, with her husband Greg. They raised three daughters and numerous cats and dogs.

Patti worked at two area history museums for thirty-two years. After retiring she finally had the time to do the thing she always wanted to do: write! She always loved reading and at each army post, and the library was the first place she'd seek out.

Patti's writing is about emotional connections, friendship and family. She was thrilled when her first novel, *Please…Tell Me More,* was published in 2020 by Blue Fortune Enterprises, LLC. Her second novel, *I'll Get By,* came out in 2022 and her third, *Stop Talking,* was released in late 2023. She's currently working on her first mystery.

Patti has had stories printed in literary journals and anthologies and one was read on a podcast. She's given talks at area libraries and writing symposiums about how to tell your story.

When not writing, Patti enjoys photographing birds on her creek. She also enjoys gardening, yoga, and researching her family on Ancestry. There are some stories there yet to be told. She and Greg love traveling and are slowly ticking off their bucket list.

You can find Patti's book on Barnes & Noble, Amazon, or wherever books are sold, and you can contact her on her website, pattiproauthor.com, email patti.pro@cox.net, or on Facebook.

"Christmas always rustled. It rustled every time,
mysteriously, with silver and gold paper, tissue paper and
a rich abundance of shiny paper, decorating and hiding
everything and giving a feeling reckless extravagance."

Tove Jansson

Christmas Eve Deer

by Susan Williamson

*M*y first semester in graduate school was pocked with upsetting news from home, 3000 miles to the east. My favorite uncle had died suddenly of heart failure. He was a large man, given to afternoon snacks of pie and ice cream. He smoked, as did my parents, and drank, although I don't think to excess. I suspect he was also my father's favorite brother. My father had six brothers who had lived to adulthood. One died in the war and one in a motorcycle wreck at a young age, but of course I never knew them.

This uncle was divorced, and my mother always invited him and his girlfriend to holiday dinners and the like. He gave us each ten dollars every Christmas. I saved mine, but my brother spent his and borrowed mine, only to be repaid when I squealed on him. Uncle Phil also gave us some kind of awful cream eggs at Easter, and we had to pretend to like them. We visited his lake cottage, rode in his boat and later in his airplane. I rode horses at his stable. My father was a talented horseman who raised and trained horses. Uncle Phil liked horses and invested in them, but never rode as far as I knew. He was a Buick dealer and let my teenaged brother drive his new car to the store whenever he visited. Fool that he was. But we survived.

I learned of his death from a phone call. But that wasn't the only news on that call. My sister, a freshman in college, had been diagnosed with epilepsy and tried to commit suicide. She had moved out of the dorm and away from home. I was in shock. My roommate, hearing my news, fixed me a strong drink.

How did I process this? I couldn't.

My sister found support through a collection of friends who embraced the convictions of a local televangelist. On one of her brief visits home, she told my mother that my mother's legs were unequal in length, but that she could fix that. My mother had never had any trouble walking, so she declined the cure. In fact, despite being only five-foot-one-and-a-half inches tall, she could out-walk most people. My sister also quit taking her prescribed epilepsy medicine, believing she was cured. That turned out to be very much not the case.

Christmas was approaching. I flew home with my beloved English Shepherd, Alfie, and watched anxiously out the window to see if his crate was transferred on the connecting flights. When my mother picked me (and the dog) up at the airport, she asked if I'd like to go to our farm for Christmas. My sister, who hated the farm, would not be joining us. My brother was married with children and living overseas. Of course I would.

We had moved from the farm, located on the outskirts of Smithfield, Virginia, where I grew up, and where we later spent wonderful weekends, to Richmond during my junior year in high school, with me kicking and screaming all the way. My father was working full time in the city and my mother was trying to save her marriage. But teenagers never see things like that. The horse farm was my identity; without it, I was a nerdy girl with a few friends and no dates.

A late bloomer, I had fallen hard in love toward the end of my senior year in college, but I left to follow my academic fellowship out west. Within a month, I received a "Dear John" letter from the object of my affections, and now, the rest of my world was falling apart.

I helped my mother stow presents and ornaments in the car, and we set off for the farm, making small talk about meals and preparations. We purchased a live tree (complete with roots, so it could be planted after), and I helped haul it into the farmhouse living room. Decorating the tree was always a Christmas Eve activity at our house. We put up the tree and my father arrived home from work in the city. My mother cooked her wonderful beef and barley soup, which we enjoyed, along with French bread from a bakery in the city and a hearty red wine. With all that was going on, my parents had to be suffering, but they made merry for my sake. I said goodnight and went up to bed around ten o'clock, while Christmas music played on the stereo.

My bed nestled between two windows which looked out on the front lawn, a generous space containing a large pine tree from a previous Christmas, huge ancient pecans, and a grassy clearing between the pine and a maple tree. It had begun to snow lightly and then more heavily after we arrived. I sat on the bed, gazing out as the moon reflected on the snowy expanse. As I watched, a small herd of deer silently wandered through the yard, a magical scene of Christmas Eve beauty and peace that conveyed, at least for the moment, that in spite of everything, all was well.

About the Author

Susan Williamson is a freelance writer, editor, and novelist. She is the author of four mystery novels and a children's book. She is the editor of *Glimpses of a Public Ivy: Fifty Years at William & Mary*. She is also a regular contributor to *Next Door Neighbors* magazine in Williamsburg, Virginia, where she lives with her husband.

Her work can also be seen in the 2024 Writers Guild of Virginia Spring Journal and several issues of Flying South, the literary anthology of Winston-Salem Writers. When not writing, she can be found riding a horse, teaching riding lessons, gardening, reading, or hanging out with friends and family. For more information go to susanwilliamsonauthor.com.

"Fine old Christmas, with the snowy hair and ruddy face,
had done his duty that year in the noblest fashion, and
had set off his rich gifts of warmth and color with all the
heightening contrast of frost and snow."
George Eliot, *The Mill on the Floss*

The Christmas Mermaid

by ML Brei

℘n the middle of a little street near the heart of Colonial Williamsburg, nestled under a chocolatier, and at the bottom of worn steps, a light shone through three circular portholes in a door adorned with nautical designs. Beyond this door was a used bookshop called Mermaid Books. And in Mermaid Books, perched on a stool behind a wooden counter, sat Nicky, a bedraggled and tired college student. She was cramming for her Poetry final exam while minding the store. This was her last shift for the semester, and she had only a couple of hours before closing time. Then exams and a long train ride home for Christmas, a lonely Christmas. Ever since learning that Brian had cheated on her…

On this chilly evening as she tried to focus on Kubla Khan and his lovely palace, four customers milled around the maze of old books and quirky merchandise. Nicky scanned the security mirrors and located each customer. A woman sat on a low stool in the children's section, book in hand, lost in story; a husband and wife were in the far corner of the store, looking over vintage postcards. And facing a shelf of history books stood a twenty-something man with a short brown ponytail and a gray scarf coiled around his neck with one end flowing down the back of his navy wool jacket.

She was not needed and went back to Coleridge. The Ancient Mariner was next up. Minutes passed.

"Why is it called Mermaid Books?" The gray-scarf man asked, startling Nicky. She looked up from her book to see the young man who had been in the history section. He had inquisitive green eyes underneath a broad forehead and a smile that on better days would have impressed her with its enchanting warmth. But tonight, it was wasted on her. She didn't have the bandwidth for nonsense.

"I don't know. Maybe the owner likes mermaids?" Nicky answered off-handedly.

"But we're in Colonial Williamsburg and this is really a great collection of great history books. And there aren't any mermaids here. They need water, right?" he said.

Nicky shut her book and sat up taller, peering directly into the young man's eyes before answering. She had no patience for the jokers who always made the same suggestions. What was his game? She flashed a grim smile at him.

She knew how to handle him. "Obviously there are mermaids here. Look around. See the big fountain in the middle of the room? Is that mermaid enough for you? And look over here and there at the mermaid signs over those books? What about these mermaid figurines, and the mermaid seashells on that shelf? Mermaid tote bags? Mermaid comics taped all over the place. Need a bottle opener? There's one over there with a mermaid handle. You want mermaids? We have mermaids. Welcome to Mermaid Books!"

"No, that's not what I meant. I know you have mermaid stuff. But shouldn't you be called Colonial Books or Ye Olde Bookshop? You know, something somewhat related to your location, your collection?"

She'd heard it all before. "Why don't you write down all the names that you think would be more fitting? I'm sure Ellie will take great interest."

The young man gave Nicky a quizzical look. "Ellie is the owner?"

"She sure is."

Nicky handed a piece of note paper and a pencil to her inquisitor, not expecting him to respond. They never did when she challenged them. "Here. Go ahead. Do your best. Why don't you suggest a contest while you are at it. We'll call it: What *not* to rename Mermaid Books!"

He glanced at her momentarily and to her surprise, took the pencil and paper and began to write. After finishing, he folded the paper lengthwise, made a triangle at one end, folded it like a flag, and ended by tucking the last bit under a flap. He handed the neat little triangle to Nicky.

"This should do it! Have a great evening," he said. He smiled once more, gave her a brief nod, and left the store.

One gone, three to go, thought Nicky as she dropped the triangle onto the countertop.

She continued to study, only stopping occasionally to check the status of her customers. She had less than an hour before closing time. If she were lucky, everyone would be out long before then.

Closing time arrived at last. She packed up, looked down and saw the triangle of paper on the counter. She slipped it into her pocket. After securing the register and turning off the lights, Nicky locked up. This was it. She wasn't sure she'd come back in January. Mermaid Books, which at first seemed so promising, now remained tethered to the rest of her misery. No happiness, no joy. She laboriously climbed the steps to the street level where a colonial-style streetlight illuminated a tall Christmas tree adorned with large red ribbons. It was the festive "holiday fur tree" that

44

Ellie put up every year to benefit the local humane society. Typically Nicky enjoyed looking at the names of the pets scribbled on each ribbon. But tonight, she observed the tree, thought nothing at all, and turned in the opposite direction toward campus. She trudged down the street and along the brick pathways that led to her dorm. She glanced at the building without feeling.

Jefferson Hall! Of course this would be where she ended up living. Not Landrum or any of the other cool new dorms. Good old austere Jefferson. It epitomized her entire semester: solid, solitary, static, dull, gray. She put her key card into the slot until she heard the familiar buzz and entered. She descended the steps to the lower level where she shared a corner room with her best friend. The long, empty corridor narrowed into a dark tunnel. This is my life, she thought—a dark, dank tunnel leading to boring, endless work. Few friends, no romance, no hints that anyone saw anything attractive about her. It all fit, she lamented to herself.

Once in her room, she considered her options. She hadn't eaten and it was only 8 p.m. But there was no time for food. She had yogurt in the fridge and a protein bar on her desk. That would have to suffice.

She threw her coat onto her unmade bed. The small triangle slipped out of the pocket and slid down her comforter and onto the floor. She watched it and scowled. What a bother, she thought. She picked it up and tossed it on the pile of trash in the wastepaper bin.

Later that evening, Nicky sat hunched in front of her desk, hair disheveled, random papers and pencils strewn about, and laptop humming away. Suddenly, the door burst open and Claire, her roommate, appeared in the doorway. With wide eyes, she stared across the room at Nicky.

Claire, never one to be patient with stressed-out friends, entered noisily and dumped her backpack with a great thud on the floor.

"Are you okay?"

"Yea, yea," Nicky mumbled. She glanced in Claire's direction, but her eyes couldn't focus on anything. She was a mess.

Claire looked around the room and noted that it was as frazzled as her roommate. She rolled her eyes. She, too, had a final the next morning but had been studying for days and was ready to call it a night.

"Hey, can I do anything?" she asked Nicky as she skirted around a pile of clothes and books on the floor. Before Nicky could answer, she spotted the overflowing trash in the wastepaper bin.

"I'll just toss this out," she said and she grabbed the bin. As she lifted it, the little paper triangle slipped out and onto the floor once more.

"Whoops!" said Claire as she picked it up.

Nicky lifted her head and turned toward her roommate,

who was holding up the triangle. "Oh. Those are names for Mermaid Books. Know-it-alls are so annoying."

"What are you talking about?" Claire asked.

Nicky pushed herself away from her desk and leaned far back into her chair until she was facing the ceiling. "Some random guy said we should call it Colonial Books or whatever. They always say something along those lines. They always want to know why it's called Mermaid Books. I don't know. Why do they bother me with that?"

"You know, I've thought that myself. Why is it called Mermaid Books? Have you ever asked Ellie? I'm sure she has a good story."

"I don't care. I'm not going back there next semester. The customers are so predictable. Although at least this one had a nice way about him. And a really cute ponytail. In a previous life, I could've fallen for him. But no, he's just annoying."

Claire tossed the triangle and caught it with the wastepaper basket. "You, with a guy? After what Brian did?" She left the room rolling her eyes, unaware that the triangle slipped out just as she was leaving.

Finals came around and left. Nicky survived, but she wasn't happy with any moment of it. There was no sense of joy or relief when it was over. She went through the motions of cleaning her room and packing up for the holidays. The next day, she would be on the train and could collapse and recoup. It was Christmas, but it wouldn't be the same this year without the boyfriend who had been always been around since early high school. She plopped on her bed and stared at nothing.

The door slammed open.

"Come on, you've gotta let it go. It's over. We're free!" Claire barked.

Startled, Nicky flinched as Claire grabbed her arm. "We're going to have a little holiday cheer before you leave. Put on your coat—we're going out. Stop being a sullen miss!"

Nicky reluctantly cooperated and slugged into her coat, just catching the hat and mittens that Claire tossed.

When they reached DoG Street, they passed Side-car Santa, standing in his motorcycle at the end of the square, merrily handing out Beanie Babies to young families crowded around him. Claire laughed and suggested jokingly that they should try to get one. Nicky shrugged.

In the twilight they passed a man attired in colonial garb bearing a flaming torch which he was touching to wood piled in a tall cresset basket. Small clusters of people stopped to watch as he patiently worked the flame and wood until at last, the wood caught fire.

As Nicky looked down the long street, she noticed the other cressets, all now lit, lining both sides. People were entering and leaving the historic sites, milling around, talking to others. Many stopped to examine the old-fashioned decorations that adorned the doors and windows of the houses. Wreaths and garlands made of pine branches and boxwood sprigs were decorated with fresh fruits and nuts, well preserved by the cold. Some of the greenery had symbolic tokens tucked into the sprigs— quills, ink wells, and parchment at the bindery; thimbles and colorful scraps of cloth at the millinery.

There were no electric lights. The street was gently illuminated in the manner of the 18th century with white candles in every window, and cressets and bonfires burning. Claire and Nicky strolled along the unpaved road, passing a horse pulling a buggy full of tourists while a small group of costumed carolers began another round of song.

Christmas should have been a joyous occasion in this picturesque setting! For Claire, it was, as she expressed through her running commentary on the unique decorations, her voice booming over the cacophony. Nicky went along, silently, focussing on avoiding contact with all merry well-wishers. She noted a small group of interpreters dressed as 18th-century townspeople standing in the middle of the road, ringing bells, laughing, greeting visitors as they passed. She navigated out of their path. Other interpreters, who also seemed eager to engage, stood sentinel near the low bonfires that provided warmth. She'd avoid them as well. She spied a split-rail fence around the colonial gardens, the length of which was clear of people. She swerved over to it. Claire followed as she continued her nonstop monologue.

As they were passing the gate in the fence, a man wearing a tricorn hat and a wool greatcoat with deep cuffs stumbled out of the gateway and collided with Nicky, throwing her off-balance.

"My apologies," he said, bowing low and displaying impeccable colonial manners. Then he looked up and saw Nicky. His eyes twinkled.

"Ah ha! We meet again!"

Regaining her composure, Nicky stared at the speaker.

"I see you've left your watery abode to grace these gardens with your sweet presence," he said.

Nicky's face turned bright red.

"May I be so bold as to inquire, have you perchance had the opportunity to visit what is known in these parts as the Holiday Fur Tree?" he asked, now openly mischievous.

Before any more words could be exchanged, a group of visitors decked out in red Santa caps converged on him and peppered him with questions about English boxwood. The girls stood for a moment watching the spectacle before moving away. Then Claire nudged Nicky.

"Do you know him? I don't. At least I don't think I know him. Who was he talking to?" she asked in a low voice.

"Me," Nicky said with eyes alight. "Let's get out of here."

Nicky steered Claire back toward campus, now in companionable silence, Claire with a quizzical look, and

Nicky with newfound energy. When they reached the tree of red ribbons, Nicky paused and started to read the names of pets. Claire followed suit.

"So, who's the guy?" Claire asked.

"No one, really. He's the triangle guy," Nicky said, now fully smiling.

Claire paused for a moment. "You mean the annoying one who you might have considered in a previous life?"

"Uh huh." Nicky spotted a ribbon. "Misha! What a perfect name for a Persian cat."

Claire looked over at the ribbon. "That's a Russian name."

"How about this one: Ivan!"

"Definitely owned by someone who works for the CIA." Both girls laughed.

And so they continued, Nicky scrutinizing the ribbons one by one.

"I wonder," she said softly.

When she reached a ribbon at the very bottom of the tree, she spotted a neatly folded triangle. On it was written in formal long-hand, "For A Mermaid". She picked it up gingerly and stared at it,

"What've you got there?" Claire asked. "Oh my gosh, another triangle? They're multiplying! You don't think it's the same guy?"

"Hmm, I think it is. And this one is not going to remain a mystery," Nicky said as she quickly unfolded it and read its contents out loud, "The Colonial Garden of Books. Yes, same guy, and another name to add to the first list."

"Not bad. A bit old-fashioned. What names did he list on the first one?"

"I never opened it. I thought I'd hang it on my Christmas tree as a reminder of my time at Mermaid Books."

"You still have it?"

Nicky withdrew a battered triangle from her pocket and held it up.

"It has a good feel to it and the lines are classic. It'll be perfect on the tree," Nicky said.

Claire shook her head, "Why don't you open it? Let's see what names he came up with. You can re-fold it, right?"

Nicky stared at the triangle that she had been carrying around, the one that she didn't want to open. Suddenly a surge of curiosity overtook her. She slipped out the top flap and gently unfurled the triangle, one side at a time, slowly. When it was fully opened, she looked down at the words. It took a moment, then her eyes welled up.

"What? What does it say!" Claire grabbed the paper. She stared at it, cocking her head to one side. She laughed and said, "No way! That would never work as a bookstore name."

Claire handed the message back to her friend, who repeated softly to herself, "You have the most beautiful smile!"

ML Brei is an accomplished writer, teacher, consultant, and small business owner. She is the author of several books including *A Different Type of Soul* (2022, Meripoint Books), *The Christian Symbols of the Twelve Days of Christmas* (2022, Meripoint Books), and *Forever Stage IV* (2023, Meripoint Books).

She is a graduate of Smith College and has three grown children. After living abroad for many years as a military spouse, she now resides in Virginia with her husband of 38 years. ML can be reached through her publisher, meripointbooks.com.

"No space of regret can make amends for
one life's opportunity misused."
Charles Dickens, *A Christmas Carol*

The Curious Case of the Christmas K9
by Narielle Living

$\mathcal{A}$ light hovered, blinking on and off, blinding her. Moaning, she tried to turn her head to escape the painful brightness. Opening her eyes, her stomach lurched. She was on the ground, outside, and everything appeared wavy, as if she were underwater. But the trees and the people surrounding her suggested otherwise. Something squirmed in her arms, and she clutched it tighter.

"She's awake," a voice yelled, as a scratchy, wet something or other swept across her face. She couldn't see the beast, but she felt the fur of whatever stood over her.

"Sherlock, leave!" a female said. She wondered who

Sherlock was and why he had to leave before everything faded to black again.

Roxie tried to ignore the constant beeping from the hospital machines. And the glare of the fluorescent lights. And the smell, which was the worst part of being in a hospital. She sat in a chair in the hallway of the emergency room at Riverside Hospital, filling out an After Action Report about the search she'd been on earlier. Her dog, Sherlock, lay on the floor next to her, ever watchful. The nurses and doctors didn't pay attention to the German shepherd, but other people often glanced at him or stopped to ask her if he was a service dog.

"Search and rescue," she explained. "So yes, he's a working dog."

One boy, around five years old, approached and grabbed Sherlock's ears before his mother could stop him. "I am so sorry!" the mother exclaimed as Sherlock sat patiently, absorbing the ear tugs with a bored expression.

Roxie smiled. "It's fine, he's trained not to react to kids, or adults, petting him." Sherlock loved kids, loved people, and absolutely loved playing. Despite his fierce look, he was in fact a big mush.

The overhead television played the news, catching Roxie's attention. "The York County Sheriff's department informed us today that they have received no credible leads in the Grinch Crimes, a series of house robberies that have occurred with the thefts being mostly Christmas presents. Police are asking anyone who may have seen anything suspicious in the Marlbank or Edgehill neighborhoods of York County last night to call 1-888-LOCK-U-UP." The reporter's voice faded as the weather person started talking about the slim-to-none possibility of a white Christmas for the southeast region of Virginia.

You're going to have some sort of karmic debt if you steal things from people at Christmas, she thought in disgust. *What is wrong with people?*

She looked up as her friend Adam plunked into the seat next to her. "Any news?" he asked.

She shook her head. "I'd hoped to be able to know something at this point. She's in and out of consciousness."

Adam studied her for a minute. "You don't have to stay here. You could go home. The search is done, and it was a success. We found her. They're both okay."

Roxie bent over to pet Sherlock. "I thought about going home but… did you see her when we carried her out? Did you hear her answers to our questions? She has no idea what happened, she's scared and alone… Besides, I've been helping take care of the little one."

Sherlock sat up, ears at attention as a nurse walked toward them. The nurse, a young woman with her brown hair pulled into a severe ponytail, smiled at Sherlock before addressing Roxie. "Hi, you came in with our new patient, Alice? She's awake and asking questions." She nodded at Sherlock. "Good thing you know dogs, right?"

Roxie ruffled Sherlock's fur, stood, and said, "I guess we better go see them. Is she okay now?"

The nurse hesitated. "Are you family?"

Before Roxie could answer, Sherlock barked. The nurse leaned over to pet Sherlock. "Are you her other puppy?"

"Uh… no. This is Sherlock, and he found Alice. We were deployed on a search after she was reported missing."

The nurse straightened. "Thank you for your work. I'm sorry, but I cannot give you any information about her condition. But like I said, she's asking questions, so you can talk to her when you go in there. The other one has made a bit of a mess, but I think we've got it cleaned up. Will your dog get along with the little one?"

Roxie nodded. "Sherlock is well trained to behave around other dogs, and he works with the dogs on his team. He's fine around puppies." She hesitated for a moment. "I took her pup out for a potty break not too long ago. What kind of a mess happened?"

The nurse sighed. "She wouldn't let that puppy out of her grasp, and we thought it best if the dog stayed with her. Then the puppy grabbed a paper cup and shredded it."

"That's not so bad," Adam said.

"Then he pulled the blanket off the bed," she continued.

"Oh," Adam said.

The nurse let out a big sigh. "Then he knocked a plant

over and spread the dirt all over."

Roxie cleared her throat to stop a laugh from escaping. Why was there a plant in that room anyway?

Roxie and Sherlock followed the nurse into the adjacent room. A yellow lab puppy, the same puppy Alice had been clutching when they found her, lay on his back, belly showing, sleeping. Roxie suppressed another smile. *Tired himself out in here.* Alice, who according to her missing person information sheet was a twenty-six-year-old Hispanic woman of medium height, sat up in bed, a vacant stare in her eyes. Her long, dark hair was matted and messy, and her dark olive complexion held a hint of gray. *I hope she'll be okay for the holidays*, Roxie thought before politely clearing her throat. The woman looked at her. "Um, hi, I'm Roxie." She stepped forward and offered her hand. "And you are Alice, correct?"

Alice's eyebrows drew together in confusion for a moment before she started screaming.

"How was I to know she'd react like that?" Roxie said at the end of the hallway after being escorted out of the hospital room. "All I did was introduce myself."

Adam sighed. "You really do not need to be here. After we find the missing, we go home."

Home was complicated, though. Home was where her little brother was crashing on her couch, fresh out of rehab and desperately trying to hold his life together and not drink again. Home was where she slept alone after saying goodbye to her boyfriend of five years, all because he wanted to start a family immediately and she was uncertain. And home was where a stack of ingredients sat in her pantry, waiting for her to make the cookies her grandmother used to make, cookies the entire family loved that her grandmother was no longer here to make.

How the hell was she supposed to face making those cookies? It was easier to avoid it.

Sherlock whined, tugging on his leash. "What's that about?" Adam asked. "He looks like he wants something."

Roxie studied her dog. "I'm not sure." She loosened her grip on the leash and, as expected, Sherlock moved in the direction of Alice's room. "Sorry, buddy, we've been kicked out of there." The dog turned and looked at her, and Roxie realized that while she had been kicked out, the dog had not. She unclipped the leash and said, "Free." Maybe Sherlock would keep the puppy in line.

Sherlock loped over to the door to Alice's room, and with one last look at Roxie, padded in.

She didn't know why she'd screamed. She didn't know much of anything, actually. When she saw that woman standing in her room, her body flooded with fear. But why? She didn't look like a dangerous person. But what does a dangerous person look like?

Her head hurt. She still could not remember anything, nothing. No memories. No name. Nothing except a puppy sitting on her chest, staring at her. She somehow remembered this was her dog, but she was too tired to think about what that meant.

Click, click, click.

What—

The other dog, the German shepherd, entered her room, nails clicking on the floor. He jumped on her bed and settled near her feet. The puppy squirmed his way over to the dog and began pushing at him with his nose. The big dog put a paw out and held the puppy down until he stopped squirming. They were still, the puppy seeming to understand that the big dog meant business. For the first time since she'd been awake, she relaxed.

A nurse, the same one who had been in earlier, bustled into the room and spotted the dog. "Oh, I don't know—"

"I need him," she interrupted, her voice raspy. "I need him to stay. He's helping."

The nurse nodded once and approached the bed, clipboard in hand. "How are you? You gave us all a scare when you started screaming."

Tears welled in her eyes. "I don't understand why I did that," she whispered.

"It's okay. Sometimes that happens. Do you remember me telling you that you have transient global amnesia?"

She shook her head. She remembered nothing.

"It's temporary," the nurse said. "It comes on suddenly, caused by things like strenuous activity or an emotional upset, some kind of bad news or conflict or even overwork. The good news is it will go away soon, and if you have a visitor such as a friend or family member, you will probably remember them."

A memory floated, wispy, but it was gone before she could catch it. "Has anyone been here? Besides… the woman I screamed at?"

The nurse stepped close to the bed. "Do you know who that person is?"

She shook her head. "No, I don't think so. But something about seeing her made me afraid… but that doesn't make sense." The machines around her beeped, monitoring her heart rate and blood pressure. The overhead light buzzed and a flurry of people fast-walked past her door. This was a hospital, so she should be safe. "Can… can you ask her to come back in? Maybe I'll remember something."

The nurse hesitated then nodded. "Okay, but I'm right here. And she's one of the good ones. Her and the big dog are with the search team who found you."

As the nurse left the room, her mind struggled to put that piece of information in the right spot. Found her? Apparently she'd been lost. And people had to find her. The big dog at the foot of the bed started to belly crawl closer to her while the puppy looked ready to pounce on something. A flash of memory… voices and fur… had the dog helped find her?

She smiled at the dog, who had inched his way up to her, lying with his head near her hand. She reached out to pet him, and he gave a big sigh. She might not remember her own name, but she knew she loved dogs.

A shadow fell across her bed. The nurse stood there, with someone behind her. "This is Roxie. She and her partner, Sherlock," she gestured to the shepherd, "found you earlier today. I'm not sure how much you remember, but Roxie and Sherlock got you and your puppy into the ambulance and then came here to make sure you were okay."

Fur. Wet kiss. Leave.

She looked up at Roxie. "Did you tell your dog to leave?"

Roxie nodded. "It's a command that tells him to stop doing something. He was licking your face, and we needed to give you medical attention."

Sherlock raised his head, looked at Roxie, and gave a small woof. The puppy jumped on Alice's legs and buried his nose in the sheets. "He is a very smart boy," Roxie said.

She needed to decide what to ask. How had she gotten here? "My name is… Alice?" she said in a small voice. "How do you know that?"

Roxie motioned to the chair next to the hospital bed. "May I sit near you?" When Alice nodded, Roxie sat down and pulled out her phone. She scrolled for a moment, then showed the phone to Alice. "Here's your info sheet that we were given prior to searching for you."

Alice took the phone and stared at it. There was a photo and information describing her. She knew that photo… it was taken… "My brother," she gasped. "I have a brother. Edward."

The nurse gave her a big smile. "Yes you do. He is on his way here right now."

Roxie leaned back. "He's the one who reported you missing. We sort of had an idea of where you went, so fortunately it was only a matter of hours before we found you. Could've been much worse. And Edward told us you had your puppy with you, and he was adamant that you wouldn't go anywhere without the puppy."

Alice handed the phone back to Roxie. "It was cold… and I was running through the woods… the dog squirmed a lot…" But why? Why was she running? For some reason, she hesitated to ask. She shivered. She must have been running from something horrible.

A man stood in the doorway, hesitant. "Roxie? I need you for a moment."

Roxie nodded and stood. "I'll be right back," she said. Alice heard her but was trying to sort through the images starting to flood her memory. Sherlock scooted closer, providing warmth and comfort as realization dawned.

Roxie stood in the hallway, trying to understand what Adam was telling her. "Why is the brother at the police station instead of here?"

Adam ran a hand through his hair, clearly disturbed. "They brought him in for questioning. There's some indication that he may have information about—"

A flash of yellow fluff came barreling toward them, paws sliding across the slick hallway. For a moment it appeared the puppy was going to career into a wall before righting himself and continuing. Roxie stepped into the middle of the hallway and crouched, holding out a dog treat. "Come, puppy." The ball of fluff crashed into her, causing her to fall backward. Puppy teeth snatched at the dog treat and Roxie grabbed him, lifting him in her arms and standing while trying not to laugh.

The nurse came out of Alice's room and hurried over to Roxie. "Thank goodness. Alice is beside herself and trying to—"

"Tucker!" Alice called, appearing in the doorway. "You are such a naughty boy!"

Roxie finally let go of the laughter she'd been holding in. "You might want to rename him, maybe call him Chase."

The elevator doors behind Roxie opened with a ping, and a moment later a young man stood next to Roxie, trying to take the puppy from her arms. "This is Alice's dog," he said. "Why do you have him?"

Roxie turned, shielding the puppy, and Sherlock bounded out of the room and came running down the hallway. He too slid on the slick floor, but this time Roxie was ready and stepped out of the way before she got knocked down again. Sherlock righted himself and stood in front of Roxie, blocking the young man.

"Edward," Alice called, standing still and looking even more pale than before.

"You know him?" Roxie wasn't handing this puppy over to anyone but Alice, no matter who he was.

Alice nodded. "He's my brother. Edward. He's the reason I ran."

Trying to control a squirming puppy, Roxie took a breath. Was Alice's brother hurting her? A sheriff's deputy stepped next to Edward and said to Alice, "Ma'am, can we go back to your room and talk?"

Edward darted over to Roxie and grabbed the puppy, snarling, "He is not your dog!" The squirming puppy licked his face and peed all over the front of his shirt.

Alice sighed. "You'd better all come to my room."

Alice had a whopper of a headache but at least her memory had returned. Both dogs lay quiet on her bed, curled next to each other. She squeezed her eyes shut.

"Edward, I don't understand why you did that."

Edward stood at the edge of her bed, shirt wet from trying to wash it out in the bathroom sink. "I—" he began, but the deputy cut him off. "Ma'am, can you tell me why you ran out of your brother's house earlier today and into the woods down the road?"

She hadn't known what to do. She'd walked into Edward's house, puppy on the leash, so excited. She had finally trained the dog to give her a high-five with his paw, which she wanted to show off to her brother, and she was supposed to help him wrap Christmas presents. But apparently he'd forgotten she was coming, because when she walked into his living room, he stood next to his friend, Jesse, arguing in low tones and gesturing at the pile of gifts on the floor. Clearly the presents had been wrapped, but the wrapping was torn and the gifts lay all over. Lots of gifts. Expensive gifts.

"I realized at that moment that my brother was…" Her sentence ended in a sob, and it took a moment for her to pull herself together. "You're the Grinch." She opened her eyes, tears streaming. "What is Mama going to say? You're going to jail!"

The deputy leaned back in his chair and took a deep breath. "Okay, thank you for the information. At this point I can tell you that your brother is definitely not the person committing the Grinch crimes. Quite the opposite."

Alice watched as Adam, Roxie, the nurse, and Edward

all exchanged looks. Only the dogs didn't seem to care what was happening. "So… you're not stealing those gifts?"

Edward looked wounded. "No, I'm a CI."

The deputy snorted. "Not anymore."

"What's a CI?" Alice asked.

"Confidential informant," Roxie said. "Your brother was helping catch the bad guys."

Alice turned to Edward, eyes shining. "So you're really a… CI?"

"I was," he answered. "I don't think I qualify anymore." He shuffled his feet, looking down. "I didn't always have the best track record of making good choices when I was young. But at some point, I realized I didn't want to do that anymore. I wanted to do better. I wanted more from life than always having to hide or lie or… whatever."

Silence hung over the room for a moment, then Alice said, "I had no idea."

Edward nodded. "So when I saw some… *activities* happening last year, I went to the sheriff's office and talked to them. This group, these guys who've been stealing, this has been going on for a long time."

"I'm going to have to ask you not to talk about that," the deputy said. "We've got a ways to go until we get through the legal system."

Edward nodded. "I want my life to mean something, to count for something. I want to help."

"The sheriff's department is hiring right now," the

deputy said. "You'd have to go through the academy and a background check, but you might want to consider it."

Edward's face lit up. "Yeah, I'll think about it."

Alice looked up at the ceiling. Her brother was right. They'd been raised by good people, raised to do the right thing and make the world a better place. "It's easy for you," she said. "Sounds like you know what you want to do. I'm still trying to figure it all out. I don't think I'd be good in law enforcement, but I'd like to do something too, something that helps people."

"You already have a job," Edward said.

Alice nodded. "Yes, but maybe I can do more."

A soft woof sounded from the bed, and Sherlock nudged the puppy, who had started nibbling on part of the sheet. Roxie laughed. "I think my dog is making a suggestion."

Alice looked at her, puzzled. "A suggestion?"

"Labs have great noses, and this one is more than playful. He just might need a job, and he could qualify as a search dog after training. *Lots* of training," Roxie said.

"A job peeing on people?" Edward muttered.

"How would I do that?" Alice asked.

Roxie signaled Sherlock to come to her. The big dog hopped off the bed and Roxie clicked the leash onto his collar. "I'll reach out to you later this week, once you're feeling better, and we can talk more. I've got to head out for now, though. I'm really, really glad you're okay." She studied Alice for a moment. "You had us worried."

"I'm going too," Adam said. "Where you headed, Roxie?"

Roxie smiled at her friend. "Sherlock and I are going home to make cookies."

Narielle Living is the president and founder of Blue Fortune Enterprises, a publishing company who believes that books have the power to change lives. She is also the managing editor for the Williamsburg, Virginia magazine *Next Door Neighbors* and has written hundreds of do-it-yourself articles for online magazines.

Narielle is the author of the mysteries *Signs of the South*, *Revenge of the Past*, *Christmas in Virginia*, *Madness in Brewster Square*, and *Birding in Brewster Square*, and she co-authored *Chesapeake Bay Karma—The Amulet*. In addition, her fiction appears in the Chesapeake Bay Writers' first anthology, *Harboring Secrets*. She edits both fiction and nonfiction and loves helping other writers achieve their goals. Narielle is currently working on her next books, which include the next mystery in the Brewster Square series and a memoir about adoption.

For more information about Narielle or her books, you can find her at blue-fortune.com.

"At Christmas every body invites their friends about
them, and people think little of even the worst weather.
I was snowed up at a friend's house once for a week.
Nothing could be pleasanter."

Jane Austen, *Emma*

Dancing on DoG Street

By Kristen M. Overman

*P*earl sipped the last of her hot chocolate and wiped the whipped cream mustache from her lip. She glanced at her phone for the hundredth time. Still no word from Dara. They were supposed to meet at the café twenty minutes ago, and once again, Dara had blown her off.

She shouldered her backpack and stepped out onto Duke of Gloucester Street. The December sun sunk low, and a cool breeze scattered some straggling oak leaves on the sidewalk. Pearl zipped her coat to her chin and looked at the Christmas baubles hanging in the windows of Brick & Vine. *I bet I could find something for Mom in there.*

Her phone buzzed in her pocket. *Finally!* She pulled it out, only to see a message about another sale at Shutterfly. *I don't have any cards to send. No updates to give people. Still living the same life, same job, same everything as last year. Sort of.*

She shoved the phone back in and continued down the street. Christmas was usually her favorite time of year. The lights, the decorations, eating crazy amounts of food with her family. This year everyone was scattered, though. Her parents had decided to leave for a cruise on the twenty-sixth, so her siblings were going to visit their significant others' families, and now her best friend was practically ghosting her. Ever since Dara and Keith had gotten together, she'd become more distant. Pearl got it. New relationships could be all-consuming. But they'd weathered high school, and college, and enough other drama that Pearl had figured they were solid—especially now that they were both back in Williamsburg.

She shuffled past the Precious Gem, barely glancing at the rings and necklaces on display. *A year ago, I was ring shopping…* She pushed the thought from her head. *Maybe that's why Dara's avoiding me. She thinks I'm still too broken up over Jeff to be happy for her. She couldn't be more wrong.*

Dating Jeff had been fun, but their relationship should have ended well over a year before it did. It had taken looking at rings to push Pearl into admitting she didn't see a future with him. She'd become the worst version of herself when they were together. *I should have known it was all wrong the second he refused to dance with me.*

Really, it was more than that. She loved the mountains, he hated the cold. She loved a good novel on a rainy day, his attention span was shorter than an Instagram reel. They'd gotten together through friends and stayed together because it was convenient. At a time when everyone seemed to be pairing off and getting married, it was nice to have a plus-one. And someone to go out with on weekends, or check in with during the day at work. *But not the right one for the rest of my life. I know better now. I hope.*

The breeze picked up, and Pearl caught the scent of waffle cones. Her stomach rumbled, but she continued on. No point going to the Cheese Shop or Kilwin's alone. Besides, it was too cold for ice cream or sitting outside to people watch. She crossed South Henry Street, headed for the Bruton Parish shop. It was always good for a few stocking stuffers for her mom. She could use another funny dishtowel. Last year's had said something like, *If eating potato chips counts, yeah, I do crunches.*

And then her phone buzzed. She reached into her pocket so fast, she almost stumbled. Dara hadn't completely forgotten her!

Hey girl, sorry I flaked on Illy. Can you meet for a quick drink at Sweet Tea & Barley instead? I'll be there in 10.

Pearl glanced at the time. She didn't have anywhere

else to be, really.

Sure! I'll walk over.

She adjusted her backpack and picked up her pace. She felt lighter.

She hustled past the Bruton Parish shop and circled around the crowd leaning on the fence to look at the horses. She hopped back onto the sidewalk and paused by the gate to Bruton Parish. Strains of organ music came out the open door. It sounded like *Hark! The Herald Angels Sing*. Pearl looked around. It was Friday. Odd time for a service, but she didn't see any cars parked, just a horse-drawn carriage making one of its last rounds of the day coming toward her.

A small bundle of white streaked out of the open church door onto the sidewalk. Without looking, it ran for the street. The horse startled, then sped forward. Pearl dropped her backpack and sprinted to grab the child before it was hit. They both fell on the curb in a pile as the horse and carriage continued on, the driver looking over his shoulder and nodding at Pearl.

"Are you okay?" Pearl leaned back to get a look at the runaway.

The child nodded and stuck a finger in his mouth.

"What happened?"

He pulled the finger out. "I wanted to get outta that stinky place."

"Henry! We were looking for you!" a deep voice boomed.

"You're supposed to be in the balcony with the rest of the angels." A tall guy with sandy hair strode toward them.

"I'm not an angel. I'm a sheep. *Baaa!*" Henry crossed his arms.

Pearl extricated herself and attempted to stand.

"Here, let me help you." The guy offered his hand. "Thanks for saving Henry here. Not sure how I would've explained that to his parents."

Pearl took his hand and stood, then brushed herself off.

"I'm Nick. The, uh, director of this year's pageant. Not exactly by choice—I just moved back to town and my mom thought I could use a little holiday service project." He grinned. "I was voluntold."

Pearl laughed. "That seems a little extra. Have you done something like this before?"

"Never. Well, not since I helped with it in youth group back in high school." He ran his hand through his wavy hair. "Are you okay? I hope you didn't get too banged up… ah…" He raised his eyebrows.

"Oh, sorry. I'm Pearl. It's nice to meet you." She extended her hand and noticed it was scraped.

"Shoot, do you need a Band-Aid?" Her hand looked tiny in his. "Come on inside and warm up… Ow!" He looked down. Henry kicked his shin again. "What was that for?"

"Stop talking to the pretty lady! She was my friend first. I bet she never woulda made me an angel!"

"I'm beginning to wonder why anyone would." Nick shook his head. "Tell you what, Henry. I think we have room for one more animal. But you look a little big for a sheep."

"*Baaaa!*"

"Never mind. Sheep it is. We'll ask Mrs. Beardsley for a different costume when we get inside."

Henry nodded. "Okay."

The organ music started again, this time with the choir accompanying it.

Pearl nodded toward the church. "Sounds like they might need you in there."

Nick looked down at her. He had soft brown eyes. "Yeah. Can I get you that Band-Aid? Maybe a glass of water?"

"No, I'll be fine. But thanks. I appreciate it." She picked up her backpack from the sidewalk and shouldered it. Nothing seemed to have fallen out.

"This might sound weird, and I promise I'm not a creep… which is probably also something a creep would say… but would you like to get coffee or something when I finish here? It would be nice to meet up with a friendly face." He smiled again, looking into her eyes.

Pearl blushed and looked away. "Um, I would, but I'm actually late meeting someone right now."

Nick's face fell. "Of course. Sure. It's Friday. You must have all kinds of plans."

"Oh, no, I'm just supposed to meet my friend for a drink

at the Lodge. Some other time, maybe?" She fumbled for her phone. She must have dropped it when she fell.

Henry tugged Nick's arm toward the church. "Come on!"

An older woman appeared in the doorway. "Nick! We need you inside now!"

"Yes, Mrs. Beardsley." He turned over his shoulder to Pearl. "Sorry, that's my cue. I hope I see you again, Pearl."

Pearl spotted her phone on the ground by the curb and picked it up. "Me too!"

But Nick had already disappeared inside.

Pearl half-smiled. *At least I know where to find him.*

She crossed the street and headed toward the path that cut over to England Street. As she approached Sweet Tea & Barley, she looked in the tavern windows and saw Dara sitting at a high top. With Keith.

Pearl's heart sank. She'd hoped to have some one-on-one time, even if it was short. Moving back here after Jeff last year had been hard. Making friends in her late twenties was more complicated than she'd thought it would be. Dara had been a bit of a lifeline, her one social connection outside of work. She mustered a smile and pushed the door open.

Dara waved her over. And then kept waving. And then shaking her hand.

Pearl's jaw dropped. The ring on Dara's finger sparkled even in the muted tavern light.

"It's official!" Dara squealed and side-hugged Keith. "We wanted to tell you in person! We've been talking about it for a while, and decided we're gonna elope in the Caribbean for New Year's!" She handed Pearl a glass of champagne, and she and Keith raised theirs.

For a while? What, two weeks? They've barely been together six months. Pearl swallowed. "Congratulations!" She raised her glass and clinked with theirs.

Dara and Keith looked into each other's eyes. "We just knew when we met this was it." Dara sighed. "We have so many plans and ideas and adventures ahead of us. Why wait? And we don't want a big expensive ordeal. Besides, you know how complicated my family is."

"And mine isn't much better," Keith said. "It would be hard for some of my relatives to travel, and I don't want them to feel like they have to get on a plane for the islands and all that. We'll have a party or something for everyone in the spring."

Pearl nodded. Dara had skipped prom and college formals, and had tried unsuccessfully to get out of being her sister's maid of honor. It made sense she'd want to elope.

"Wow. I'm so… happy for you. I don't know what to say. It's just—"

"Sudden, I know. I get it. This is why we're telling you first. We need to practice for when we tell our families." Dara leaned into Keith and held his hand on the table.

"It will be perfect, wherever we go." He wrapped his other arm around her shoulders.

"Is there… is there anything I can do to help?" Pearl looked from Dara to Keith and took another sip.

Dara shook her head. "Not now. But when we figure out the party, we'll take whatever help we can get."

Pearl swirled the champagne in her glass. "Let me know your theme or whatever and I'll run with it."

"We so appreciate it, Pearl!" Dara eyed Pearl, reached across the table, and took her hand. "You need to get out more, meet other people. You've done enough time solo."

Pearl half-smiled. "I'm good. I know myself better than I did a year ago. And I'm figuring the rest out."

"Yeah you are!" Dara grinned. Her phone buzzed on the table and she turned it over. The screen was lit up with notifications. She nudged Keith. "Babe, we need to roll. They're all waiting for us at Craft 31."

Keith stood and helped Dara to her feet.

Pearl raised an eyebrow. "What's up?

"Oh sorry, it's a thing for a guy Keith works with. We said we'd be there earlier, but I wanted to see you first." Dara fluffed her hair as Keith helped her with her coat. "We'll talk soon, okay?"

"Sure."

Keith dropped some bills on the table. "That should cover it. Thanks for coming, Pearl. Sorry we have to run out."

Pearl watched them leave, then looked back at the three

glasses of champagne. She took a slow sip of hers. *Dara is getting married. To Keith. Soon.* She took another sip. She'd never had that feeling with Jeff. She'd hoped, especially in the beginning when everything was new. But when she was being honest with herself, she knew. She knew she was forcing it to work. She knew she wanted no part of parenting with him. And she knew the more time they were together, the worse she felt about herself and him. The breakup wrecked her more because of the changes it forced. She moved, started a new job—and there was no one to share it all with, to talk to at night, to go out and socialize. Some parts of life were just easier as a couple.

Dara, though… Pearl smiled. She had her head screwed on. If she said she knew, there was no doubting the decision.

Pearl took a last sip of champagne and counted the bills Keith had left to make sure they would in fact cover the tab, then stood and shrugged her coat on. She shouldered her backpack and headed back out into the crisp air. The gaslight styled street lamps glowed in the dusk as she retraced her steps back to DoG Street.

I definitely know what I don't want. She shook her head. No more thinking about Jeff tonight. She had to look forward. *I want someone who likes to read actual books, not a Kindle. Someone who pays attention to the world and likes to talk about it, more than what they see on social media … And someone who will dance with me the second a song comes on that hypes me up.*

Pearl reached the path back to DoG Street and looked up at the Bruton Parish spire. Maybe Nick was still there, and they could get that coffee. She felt a surge of champagne confidence. He seemed like a good guy. He had to be, to work with a pack of feral kids in the week before Christmas.

But as she got closer to the church, she saw all the lights were out, doors closed. She slowed her pace. Nothing to hurry toward now. She should've followed him in. Let him get that Band-Aid. *Dara's got it right. I need to take more chances.*

Pearl stared up at the church. She'd been in Christmas pageants as a kid, too. Never scored the role of Mary, that went to her sister. Her favorite part had been as Innkeeper Number Two. She'd had one line, "No room, no room, sorry, no room!" It had become a family refrain over the years. No room at the inn. She smiled. For all their complaining at the time, the pageants had been fun. Running around the church, playing with the three-way mirrors in the ladies' room, getting into the costume bins. They'd moved to Williamsburg in middle school, and she'd never gotten involved with a church group again.

She sighed and continued walking up the street. *Might as well get some shopping done.* The Bruton Parish shop was still lit up, so she plodded up the stairs and pulled open the heavy door.

"Merry Christmas!" the older lady behind the counter called out. "You're in luck—we extended our hours tonight. People seem to enjoy wandering in from the skating rink to shop while their kids are on the ice."

Pearl smiled back. "Thanks. I'm looking for stocking stuffers."

"Mm-hm. We have those! Try down the hall there, dear." The woman gestured to Pearl's right.

Pearl made her way through the display detailing the parish history into a narrow hallway filled with Christmas tree ornaments on one side and knickknacks on the other. She found one mini tree covered in different types of fluffy owls. Her sister would love them—but she couldn't decide on one, so she picked three. Then she found a bag of licorice that looked like coal. Perfect for her brother.

Arms full, she saw the door to the chapel was open and stepped inside. Candles were lit by the altar, and soft music played. It sounded like an instrumental version of "Oh Come, Oh Come, Emmanuel." She sat in one of the small pews and closed her eyes. The effects of the champagne had waned. She breathed deeply and pictured Christmas mornings through the years, with all of her family together. *I know nothing stays the same forever. I'm sad this had to change, though.* But maybe it would just be for this year. She'd still see her parents Christmas morning, before they left for the airport. *I should offer to drive them to Richmond. It'll be easier for them, and then we can have a little more time together.*

Pearl inhaled again and felt the tension in her shoulders fade. *Maybe I should find a church. That would be a good start to finding my people.* Not Bruton, though. The pews were too uncomfortable. *It's time I start creating my own opportunities. I'll push myself to do more on my own. I don't need Dara to invite me somewhere to make things happen.*

Everything will get better.

She opened her eyes and gathered her things. She tiptoed out of the chapel and back into the crowded hallway, then made her way to the cash register.

"Find everything you were looking for?" The elderly cashier raised her eyebrows.

"I did, thank you."

"This is a special place, isn't it?" The cashier nodded. "Oh, and I just love these owls! So soft!" She wrapped them in tissue. "Are they for you or someone else?"

"They were for my sister, but now I'm thinking I'll keep one for myself. A little reminder that wisdom can be found almost anywhere, when you let yourself hear it." Pearl swiped her credit card.

The cashier beamed. "Exactly!" She handed Pearl the package. "You never know what the next moment might bring. You have a Merry Christmas!"

"Thanks, you too. I really do love your shop here." Pearl pushed on the heavy door.

"So do we, darlin', so do we!"

DoG Street was now fully dark. The skating rink in the middle bustled with winter-coat clad figures circling around, bathed in white Christmas lights. The speakers blared *Have a Holly Jolly Christmas!* Pearl looked around and felt like part of the crowd, caught up in the momentum of music and skating. On a whim, she tucked her package into her backpack and made her way to the skate rental booth.

The music changed as she stood in line. She listened to the first few notes: *I Gotta Feeling*, by the Black Eyed Peas. *I thought they only played Christmas music here. But this hypes up the vibe.* She bounced to the beat, looking at the assortment of skates. Then she felt a tap on her shoulder.

"Pearl? Is that you?"

She turned to see Nick standing in line behind her, grinning.

"Oh! Hey, Nick, yeah, it's me." *Use your words, Pearl. Come on.*

"I can't believe it's you! I ran back out after I got Henry inside but you'd already left. Sorry about that. I didn't mean to leave you hanging."

Pearl smiled. She felt her shoulders moving to the music. She couldn't help herself. "No worries! I'm so glad you're here. I walked past the church on my way back but everything was already closed up."

Nick bounced a little, too. "I really love this song. It makes me dance wherever I am. Sometimes it's a problem when I'm driving." He raised his eyebrows at her. "Are you here with your friend?"

"Um, no. No. She and her fiancé had somewhere else to be."

"Oh! That's great! I mean, maybe great. For me. What I mean is, I'm here solo, too. I had to hang out until the older kids were picked up, but they've all left now. I'm babbling, sorry. What I'm trying to—"

"Hey Nick, would you like to skate with me?" Pearl smiled up at him.

"Yes. Most definitely. But only if we can keep dancing like this."

Pearl nodded. "I wouldn't have it any other way."

"Tonight's gonna be a good night," faded from the speaker, followed by more Christmas music. Pearl and Nick got their skates, laced up, and stepped onto the ice.

Pearl wobbled, caught herself, and wobbled again. "It's been a few years."

Nick took her elbow. "I've got you."

"How do you skate so well?" She tried not to clutch his arm too tightly.

"Years of hockey practice. But it was never really my thing. I was more of a tech guy. You know, tinkering with things, reading a lot of sci-fi and Stephen King."

Of course. Pearl felt warm. *I don't know where this guy came from, but my eyes are wide open.*

Nick picked up their pace, then held Pearl at arm's

length. "Do you trust me?"

Pearl laughed. "Sure!"

He twirled her in close, then let her spin out and back to him. She threw her head back and laughed again. "You've got some moves!"

Nick winked. "I bet the kids wish they were as cool as us!"

"Ha! I doubt it, but I'm not complaining."

They circled the rink several more times, then collapsed on a bench, winded.

"That was the most fun I've had in a long time. Thank you!" Pearl leaned back on the bench, willing her breathing to slow down.

"Me too." Nick turned to look at her. "I don't suppose you'd like to get something to eat after this?"

"I'd love to." Pearl stood. "But first let's keep dancing."

Kristen Overman is an editor and book coach for Good Story Editing. She edits all genres of novels, memoirs, outlines, and picture books, and coaches clients through all phases of their writing journey, from outline to drafts to submission. Her BA is in English and Political Science, and post-grad she took classes in Advanced Memoir and Writing the Novel at Harvard.

A member of Chesapeake Bay Writers, Virginia Writers Club, James River Writers, and formerly of SCBWI and the Writers Loft (MA), Kristen began her journey writing for kids and young adults, and has since pivoted to clean romance and collaborative projects.

When not writing, reading, or editing, she can be found outdoors, dreaming of returning to the mountains or the beach for new adventures. She lives in Williamsburg, Virginia, with her family. You can find her on Instagram @kristen_overman, X @kris10edits, or follow what she's reading on Goodreads (Kristen Overman). And if you need a little help with your story, visit https://www.goodstoryediting.com/kristen.

"It being Christmas eve, there was, as I had forseen, a
great deal of revelry and what not."
P.G. Wodehouse, *Jeeves and the Yule-Tide Spirit*

Holiday Haircuts

by Denise DeVries

Jack Duncan always began his anecdotes by saying, "I remember it like it was yesterday." The Holiday Haircut story was reserved for new customers, slow days, and long shaves. It was perfect for the smiling, portly gentleman "just passing through."

"…like it was yesterday…" Jack stopped, scissors poised. "You sure you want to get rid of the whole beard?"

The man nodded.

"No mustache, no mutton chops, just clean shaven all over?"

He nodded again.

Jack began snipping. "Let's see now, I was about ten, so it must have been 1885. That's right. Grover Cleveland was president." As his story grew, snowy hair drifted to the floor.

"I remember I had decided to practice my penmanship by writing letters to Santa Claus all summer long. On a July hot day like today, my Daddy'd had enough, so he started the holiday haircut tradition.

"He said, 'Son, you're using up every bit of paper in the house asking a man who doesn't exist to bring you things nobody can afford. I'll make a deal with you.'"

Jack examined the scissors and wiped the blades. He held them up to the light, then switched to another pair.

"Now here's the important part of the story, see? Up till then, my Daddy never wanted me underfoot in the shop. He always said, 'no son of mine is growing up to be a barber. You're going to college no matter what.'

Jack shook his head. "But that day, he took me down to the shop, got a broom, and showed me how to use it. Sure, it looks easy. But you just try handling fine curls like yours. Slant the bristles the wrong way or put too much English on it and I tell you, you'll be spitting hair for months.

"Daddy said, 'you want to celebrate the holidays in a big way. Fine. You should earn the money yourself. You can help in here after school and on weekends, and when you're twelve, I'll let you look for a summer job.' He took a big ol' jar and put a penny in it. 'You'll get one of these for every hour you work.' Now remember, a haircut cost about a dime then, so that seemed pretty generous."

Jack took a comb and straightened a curly section before snipping again. He dropped the curl on the floor and touched his own balding scalp with a sigh.

"When we told Mama about it that day at dinner, she took out an old Christmas card envelope and wrote 'Jack's Holiday Fund' in her fanciest writing, and we propped it up against the jar.

"The customers got curious, and once Daddy told them the story, they would put in a penny whenever they could spare one. I counted those coins all summer and fall thinking about what I would buy for myself. Then, a couple of weeks before Thanksgiving, old Mr. Bascombe down at the Clarion needed a story for the paper, so he wrote it up and printed a photo of me holding the jar. We still have the clipping somewhere.

"Anyway, Mr. Bascombe got the wrong end of the stick, or maybe my parents put him up to it, but when the story came out, it sounded like those pennies were for the 'less fortunate.' I didn't know how anyone could be less fortunate than I was right then, but I was about to find out."

The barber took a step back and looked at his customer, who appeared to be half-dozing in the chair. He walked around to the other side and began cutting again.

"I couldn't hardly make out the editor to be a liar, so I

had to go along with the whole thing. Still kind of makes me mad sometimes, until I think about how bad off people were back then. Why, there were some children who only went to school until they outgrew their shoes and had to pass them on to the next child in line.

"After the article came out in the paper, I got head pats, handshakes, and pennies everywhere I went. Pretty soon, people started dropping off canned goods and homemade hats and mittens at the shop, and some other people sent notes about their needy neighbors. My teacher liked the idea and got the whole class involved in distributing the gifts. It got to be a tradition, and now the Jack Frost fund is so big it has its own board of directors."

Jack started swooshing the brush around the shaving soap to make a lather. The customer asked, "Do you remember what you asked Santa for in your first letter?"

Jack covered the customer's face with lather, thinking, *he really looked better with that beard.* "How could I remember what I wrote so many years ago?" As he thought, he moved the brush as if to trace images on an invisible canvas.

The customer prompted, "Was it a bicycle? Or maybe a sled?"

"Not in the first letter. Those came later." He took the razor and began near the man's ear. "Sure, I remember now! I asked for a Gold Eagle dollar, thinking I could use it to buy everything I wanted."

"Seems sensible."

"But then I thought it would look mighty sad and lonely under the tree, and it could get lost in a stocking. Besides, I probably wouldn't want to spend one if I had it."

The customer fell silent as Jack began shaving around his upper lip, and he didn't speak again until the hot towel was on his face. "Letters to Santa are much more common these days than when you were a boy. I've even seen them published in weekly newspapers."

"Is that so?"

"Doesn't seem right somehow, publishing private communications that way. And think of the pressure on the parents." The towel slipped down his red face as he shook his head. "The whole town would be watching to see which children receive what they want."

Jack took the towel the rest of the way off. "I guess that's true."

"And those 'naughty' and 'nice' labels are so unfair. What kind of saint would refuse a child a gift just for getting into a bit of mischief?" The man's bushy white brows drew together over his nose.

"Nothing much we can do about it, is there?" Jack slapped some bracing cologne on the customer's rosy cheeks, making his whole face jiggle.

"You'd be surprised how one or two people can change a tradition." The man turned his head back and forth to see in the mirror and stroked his bare chin.

"Anything else I can do for you? Trim those brows, maybe?"

"No thanks, Jack, you've done plenty." He heaved himself out of the chair and patted his pockets. "There you go." He pulled out a coin and put it on the counter. "Keep the change, son."

Busy with the razor and towel, Jack didn't turn to look at the money. "Come and visit us again."

"Sure will. Every year, like always."

"But you've never been here before!"

The bell swung gently over the door to the empty shop, and Jack turned around His hand hovered over the gold coin gleaming on the counter. In the distance, he heard a laugh and the sound of sleigh bells.

Translator and poet Denise DeVries returned to fiction writing after joining the Tempe Public Library writing workshops in 2017. In 2019, Denise moved back to the rural Virginia town that inspired "Hull Crossing Chronicles", her historical fiction series, and "Key to History", her middle grade time travel books.

Denise wrote the one-act plays *A Two-Faced Spinster* and *Barbershop Gossip* in honor of Tempe Library Readers Theater, of which she was a member for one season. The characters and situations in the plays are inspired by her fiction.

Find out more about Denise at: www.denisedevriesauthor.wordpress.com.

"I ask you to answer me fairly: is not additional eating an ordinary Englishman's ordinary idea of Christmas day?"
Anthony Trollope, *Orley Farm*

by Narielle Living

"Try not to kill us, okay?" Angela shifted in her seat, noting the high speed her partner was driving and the icy roads. The snow had stopped falling, which was a relief, but the temperatures remained stubbornly low. In this part of Virginia, snow rarely happened, and ice was just as uncommon. Yorktown, Virginia, was known for history not snowfall.

"What?" Noah asked, a brief smile crossing his face. "You worried?"

"Yes."

"Me too," he said. "But if I go any slower, our fine

citizens will complain about how long it took us to get there. And the sheriff's department is here for the people."

York County, Virginia, did not have a police department. Instead, they had a sheriff's department, and both Angela and Noah had worked as deputies there for several years.

"If we wind up in a ditch and unable to exit our vehicle, they'll really have something to complain about."

Finally they arrived at the entrance to a suburban neighborhood. All the houses looked similar—two-story structures in muted colors, gabled roofs, and two-car garages. This time of year, holiday decorations were displayed in the front yards—snowmen and reindeer and Santas. The house they stopped at, however, had a display of the Eiffel Tower, which Angela decided not to analyze. Lights flashing, Noah left the car running as they got out and made their way down the sidewalk that had not been shoveled.

An older man opened the door before they even got there. "Took you long enough," he said. "Damn kids are going through the neighborhood again, ringing doorbells and running away. This is the third time this week, and I'm sick of it."

"Yes sir," Angela said, taking out a notepad and pen. "Approximately how long ago did this happen?"

"It's been almost an hour," he complained.

"Has anyone else been in your yard?" she asked.

"Who the hell would go out on a day like this?" he

barked at her. "It's too dangerous."

Noah and Angela exchanged glances. Apparently law enforcement didn't count when it came to going out in dangerous conditions.

She put her notepad back in her pocket. "If you'll just give me a few minutes, I think I can get this cleared up." She then followed the footprints that had been left in the snow, tracking the criminal until the footsteps ended two houses over, and knocked on the back door.

Angela was glad she'd been able to keep a straight face while she had a serious talk with the teenager who'd rung his neighbor's doorbell and thought he'd gotten away with it. "At least we know he's not going to be a master criminal," she said to Noah, not bothering to wipe the grin away. "The kid didn't even think about the tracks in the snow."

Noah snorted. "We probably just gave him his first training. Now he'll become a career doorbell ringer, striking only when the weather is perfect."

Their laughter was interrupted as the radio came to life. "Unit 105, we have a 10-67 in progress." A call for help.

"That's us," Angela said. "Let's go."

Noah groaned. "I know that address, and it's in the upper part of the county. She keeps calling."

"Doesn't matter, let's go."

Noah shifted the car and drove slowly this time. Snow had started falling again and the ice had gotten worse. The windshield wipers beat out a steady rhythm as they made their way back to Route 143. "She has dementia or something. We've been through this with her a few times already."

Angela didn't care what Noah thought. A call had gone out for a person who needed help, and that was their job. Her adrenaline had spiked. When someone needed help, it could be anything from their cat had gotten out of the house to being held hostage by a gunman. Angela hoped it would be a simple call, but she knew better than to make an assumption, no matter what Noah said. She had to go in with no preconceived ideas, alert and ready for anything, or she might not make it out.

They pulled in front of the home without lights or siren. Surrounded by acres of dense woods, the house was a craftsman-style bungalow. Cream-colored siding was complimented by dark green shutters. The fallen snow with no tire tracks or footprints coupled with darkened windows and no car in the driveway gave the place an empty appearance. This time, there were no holiday decorations, either.

Noah radioed their position, letting dispatch know they were approaching the door. Angela and Noah walked up the steps to the front porch, Angela turning sideways and knocking on the door. A white man, who looked to be in his thirties, opened the door and stepped outside. Short dark hair, pockmarked skin and average height, he was the kind of person who could be described as forgettable. "Can I help you?" he asked.

"We received a call from this address," Angela said. "From a woman who said she needed help. We'd like to come in and check on her."

The man smiled. "I'm guessing that was my grandmother. She's done that before." He turned, partially opened the door, and called, "Grandma, we have visitors!" He gestured them inside and lowered his voice. "She has Alzheimer's."

Noah nodded, stepped next to Angela, and wiped his boots. "I know. We've been here before. How's she doing?"

Angela entered, not bothering to wipe her feet. "What is your name, sir?"

He looked at her and smiled, reminding Angela of a viper. "Pete." He held out his hand. "Nice to meet you, officer."

She shook his hand and had to resist the impulse to wipe her hand clean on her pants. Bells were going off in her head but she needed to stay calm. She couldn't help anyone if she flew off the handle and tackled this guy to the ground. "Can we see your grandmother, please?"

"Of course." He led them through the front hallway and into what she guessed was the living room. It was difficult to see anything, as the curtains were drawn and there were no lights on. A heavy-set woman with short, tightly curled gray hair sat in a recliner, eyes closed.

"Ma'am?" Angela called.

The older woman slowly appeared to wake up and squinted at them. Her beady, dark eyes narrowed. "Are the Russians coming?"

"No ma'am," Noah shouted. "You're fine. We're just making sure everything is okay."

"She's old, not deaf," Angela muttered to her partner. She addressed the woman in the chair. "Ma'am, can you tell me your name?"

The woman glared at her. "I know you're here to steal my husband, ya hussy. Now git!" She nodded at Noah. "He can stay, though. He's sweet."

Pete the grandson moved to stand next to the older woman. "These nice people are here to make sure you're okay, grandma."

Her brow wrinkled in confusion. "Okay? Are we going to have a tea party today?"

Pete put a hand on his grandmother's shoulder. "If that's what you want, then that's what we'll do. Do you want cake?"

"Yes!" the woman barked. "Chocolate and vanilla!"

"Okay, let me talk with these folks first then I'll get your cake." Pete gave her another pat on the shoulder, switched the TV on with the remote, and turned the volume up loud. The older woman stared at the television, transfixed.

"I need her to tell me her name," Angela said to Pete over the blare of a commercial. "Can you give us a moment with her?"

Pete shook his head. "You seem to upset her. Maybe the other officer can talk to her?"

Angela tamped down a feeling of irritation. It would make sense that he didn't want to deal with a tantrum from his grandmother, but she really wanted at least a minute alone with the woman.

"I've been here before," Noah said. "I know her and she knows me. She looks fine, so we'll just get out of your way. I'm sorry to bother you. I know dealing with this kind of thing is always difficult."

Pete ushered them back into the hall, where Angela stopped. Framed photos in various sizes were arranged on the wall. A group of people dressed in sixties-era bell-bottom jeans and flower shirts stood in front of what looked like an old building. In one, she could just make out a sign that said *The Wharf.* "What did you say your grandmother's name is?"

Pete hesitated. "Jewel. Her name is Jewel."

Angela nodded. "And what was she doing before we got here?"

Pete shrugged, a look of amusement crossing his face. "I thought she was taking a nap, but apparently she was calling you."

Noah caught her eye, giving her a look that

communicated he didn't think they needed to dig any further. "Thanks for your time, Pete. Here's my card if you have any questions."

As they started to leave, Angela turned back to Pete. "Do you have a vehicle?"

Pete ran a hand through his short hair. "What? Why?"

"I'm just wondering. I didn't see a car in the driveway."

Noah glanced at her, clearly annoyed at the delay. A brief silence fell. "Do you have a vehicle, sir?" Noah asked.

Pete shook his head and shrugged. "No, we don't really need one. We get grocery deliveries because I don't want to be away from grandma for too long."

Angela stared at him. "How do you get your grandmother to the doctor?"

Irritation flashed across his face, replaced quickly with a smile. "I have a friend who gives us a ride when we need it. Don't worry about us, we're fine. Thank you for coming to check. I'll keep a better eye on her so she doesn't bother you anymore."

As they left, the door closed behind them with a solid thunk.

"Sarge?" Sergeant Collins looked up as Angela stood in the doorway. Her shift had ended and she found him in his shared office. Seargent Lawton was in there as well and gave her a small nod. "Can we talk?" she asked.

Sergeant Collins was her supervisor, and as far as bosses went, he was generally even-tempered and fair. "What's up, Angela?"

Angela shifted from foot to foot, knowing her superior would listen to her but the person he shared an office with… well, it would be interesting.

"Sir, I wanted to talk about a call we were on earlier today. It was a call for help from an elderly woman in the upper part of the county."

Sergeant Collins frowned. "Was it the woman with Alzheimer's? Julie?"

"Yes sir, her name is Jewel."

He nodded. "She's called a few times before. Everything go okay?"

This was where it got tricky. She didn't want to come across as hysterical or oversensitive, but she had to say something. "I'm not sure. On the surface, yes, everything was fine."

"So what's the problem?"

"Her grandson was there, and he… I don't think everything is exactly what it seems. Nothing he said, but more of what he didn't say and a really weird feeling I got about him."

Her sergeant nodded. "Okay, I hear what you're saying. Listen, if you think there's something going on, go ahead and look into it more. But do it on your own time, okay? I'm not approving overtime."

Lawton snorted. "Seriously? You had a feeling? What did your partner say?"

Angela blushed, wishing he hadn't asked. "He said things seemed okay to him."

"Then there's your answer. Leave it alone. No need to waste your time. It's almost Christmas, you probably have some shopping to do."

She knew he would say that. She also knew the best way to sidestep him and smiled. "I'm making cookies later this week. I'll save you some."

Both men visibly brightened at her before she left. She'd gotten what she had come for: permission to investigate what was really happening to Jewel.

Yorktown, Virginia, was known as the birthplace of the United States, but the upper portion of the county bore little resemblance to the historic village where tourists flocked. Closely connected to Williamsburg, the upper county was slightly more rural and often homes were far apart, as was the case with Jewel's house. Angela wasn't sure what she was looking for, but she felt compelled to check up on the house that night.

Earlier, she'd had dinner with her parents and siblings. They lived in a section of York County known as Grafton, where Angela had grown up. Her parents had the house decorated for the holidays, with outside blinking lights that would rival any airport runway and a tree laden with decorations she and her siblings had made throughout their childhoods. It was a typical middle-class home, warm and inviting, and that evening's dinner of lasagna reminded Angela how much she loved spending time with her family.

Family is important, she thought, flashing back to the cold feeling she'd had in Jewel's house. Although he'd said all the right things, she still wasn't sure that Pete, Jewel's grandson, could be trusted.

As they were finishing dinner, Angela had asked, "Does anyone here know anything about a restaurant called The Wharf? I think it used to be in Hampton." She'd done a brief online search to see what she could dig up but hadn't had much time before dinner.

"I remember that place," her mother said with a faraway look in her eyes. "Your father and I used to go there for the jazz bands."

"Yeah, the music was incredible. They had some great acts there," her father added. "Everything from jazz to blues to rock and roll. Sometimes it got crazy but it was a different era. I was sorry when it sold. I don't think they have music there like they used to."

Angela put her fork down and pushed her plate away. She knew this was a shot in the dark, but she had to try. "Do either of you remember a woman by the name of Jewel?"

Her parents looked at each other, then at her. "Jewel

was the owner," her mother said.

"One of the owners," her father corrected. "I think her parents were partners with her, but I'm sure when they passed it all came to her. They were loaded. Why are you asking?"

Angela's mind whirled, trying to figure out if this information could be useful. "I… I met her today. On a call."

Her mother sat forward, folding her arms on the table. "My goodness, I haven't thought about Jewel in a long time. She was quite beautiful. We used to wonder why she stayed here, why she didn't go off to New York or Los Angeles. How is she? I hope everything is okay."

"Beautiful?" Angela echoed. Thinking back to the woman she'd met earlier, she would not have described her as beautiful. Then again, people changed as they aged. "When was the last time you saw her?"

Angela's mother wrinkled her brow. "Last year? Dan, how long ago was it?"

Her father nodded. "Yes, we saw her last year at the Christmas tree lighting in Yorktown. Said she was remodeling her house. Putting in new hardwood floors, I think."

Her brother held up his phone. "There's a photo of The Wharf on the Remember Hampton social media page. Is this the place?"

Her mother pulled her glasses off her head and put

them on, taking the phone and staring at it before breaking into a smile. "Yes, and there's Jewel!"

When Angela took the phone, she saw it was the same photo that had been hanging in the front hallway at Jewel's house. "Which person is Jewel?"

Her mother leaned over and pointed at a young woman in the photo. Tall, with long, wavy dark hair, Jewel reminded Angela of Sofia Vergara. "That one. You can't tell from the photo, but her eyes are a striking light blue. She used to wear clothes that matched her eyes."

Angela stood. "I have to go. Sorry about the dishes."

Now here she was, unsure what to do. She parked down the street, not wanting to alert the inhabitants that she was outside. It was dark, with a deep cloud cover from the earlier storm. Clearly Pete was not a fan of Christmas, as there were no holiday lights hung either inside or outside. When she got close to the house, she skirted around a few trees and entered the backyard.

Something strange was happening. A peculiar light flickered on the ground, then the tree trunks, flashing and disappearing repeatedly. It took her a moment to realize the source: something from an upstairs window. Somebody was signaling.

What is your ETA? she texted.

Ten minutes.

No time. I'm going in.

You better be sure about this. Alzheimer's makes people do crazy things.

She shoved her phone in her pocket, ignoring the multitude of vibrations from incoming text messages.

They were going to know, at some point, that she had been in the yard. With the recent snow, her footsteps were everywhere. She thought of the young criminal they'd talked with earlier and couldn't help a small grin. At least she knew she was leaving evidence of her location. She stopped and turned her flashlight on, aimed it at the upstairs window, and blinked it on and off a few times. As she lowered it, the beam illuminated a blue tarp, which had been thrown over a large object. An object shaped like a car.

She glanced around, making sure nobody was outside, and approached the vehicle. It had been parked against the back of the house, out of sight from anyone in the front. She lifted the tarp to see the Virginia license plate, took a photo, and texted it to Noah.

This is in the backyard, she texted with the photo.

I thought he didn't have a car. Where are you?

Outside.

Stay put. I'm almost there.

But the flashing from the second floor concerned her.

What if someone was actually hurt in there?

Turned sideways, hand to hip, she quietly climbed the steps up to the front porch. The front of the house was dark, but she could barely make out a dim light in the back. As she raised her hand to knock, a blinding light came on over her head and the front door flew open.

"Well, officer, how nice of you to stop by." Pete stood in the doorway, appearing taller than he had earlier that day. "How can I help you? Or maybe I should ask, why are you creeping around my property? Do you have a warrant to do that?"

She lowered her arm slowly, squinting in the glare of the light. "Not creeping, Pete. Just checking to make sure everything is okay here."

He nodded, looking her up and down. "And what do you think, officer? Is everything okay?"

A bad feeling settled in the pit of her stomach but she tried to ignore it. "That's why I'm here. How's your grandmother? Can I come in and say hello?"

"I thought we were going to have a part-ay!" yelled a female voice from behind Pete. Angela shifted to look around him and saw a familiar woman. Her brown eyes widened. The only thing she was missing was the gray curls.

The door slammed in her face and a lock clicked.

Angela ducked low and ran around the house, where Pete and the woman from inside were pushing out the back door.

Angela drew her weapon, aimed, and in a steady voice yelled, "Freeze!"

They didn't. They did, however, get tangled in the blue tarp in their haste to take it off the car in the back, and by the time they got untangled from the tarp, Noah and a team of other officers had them surrounded.

Sergeant Collins was there, and Angela nodded at him. "Sarge, I'm going in to find Jewel."

"Noah, back her up," he barked. "Don't either of you try to be a hero."

At her insistence, Noah followed Angela up the stairs inside the house. They stayed against the wall to the edge of the stairs, trying not to be a target in case anyone else was in the house. At the top, she hesitated. Left? Right? A muffled sound came from the right, a thumping noise. Angela and Noah exchanged a look and approached the closed door.

Thump, scrape scrape. Thump, scrape scrape.

Angela knocked on the door and yelled, "Sheriff's department, is anyone in there?"

A muffled voice sounded, along with more thumps. She tried to turn the knob, but it was locked.

"Stand back," Noah ordered. "I'm going to break the door down."

Angela shook her head. "I don't think—" But it was too late. Noah had thrown himself at the door, only to bounce right off it again. She sighed, pulled out her multi-tool, flipped open the flathead screwdriver and used it to unlock the door. "You okay?" she called over her shoulder to Noah, who sat on the floor stunned and rubbing his shoulder.

He stood. "Let's see who's in there."

"I'm so glad I didn't have to break Czechoslovakian Santa," Jewel said as she sat at the kitchen table sipping her tea. "I was prepared to do just that but I didn't want to. It had belonged to my grandmother."

Angela tried to get the conversation back on track. Talking to Jewel was like following a kitten who was chasing a laser light. She was all over the place. "Can we go back to the beginning? How did you end up locked in a room and tied to a chair?"

"Two different things, darling. I was only locked in the room at first," she said. "Getting tied to a chair happened recently. I think because of your visit." Jewel smiled at her. "They knew you would find me and they panicked, I believe."

Sergeant Collins strode into the room. "Ms. Winters,

we are so glad you're okay. Are you sure you don't want to go to the hospital to get checked out?"

Jewel shook her head. "No, I'm fine. All I need is for those criminals to be put behind bars." She glanced at Noah. "Perhaps this young man should have his shoulder looked at, though. The doors here can be quite sturdy."

Noah blushed. "I was trying to—"

"You were quite gallant," Jewel said, smiling warmly. "Anyway, that awful man… Darren? Yes, Darren."

"Do you mean the person calling himself Pete?" Angela asked.

"Yes. His real name is Darren. He was one of the workers who installed new floors in the back of the house. That's how he came to know that I lived alone. And that hussy… Priscilla? Princess? What the heck was her name?"

"Phoenix," Sergeant Collins answered. "We finally got it out of her after we confiscated her identification."

Jewel gave a snort. "Oh yes, such a lovely name. She was the worse of the two. They showed up one day, bullied their way in the door and just stayed. She came up with the idea to tie me up after I called 911 the last time."

That was the one thing Angela couldn't figure out. "How did you manage to call us? Did you have a phone in the room?"

A moment of silence passed as Angela, Noah, and Sergeant Collins leaned forward to hear the answer. Finally, Jewel said, "I suppose it won't hurt to tell you since I am not a criminal." She sighed and looked up. "Back when I owned The Wharf… oh, those days were so much fun. Lots of hard work, but well worth it. The music! Anyway, as you can imagine, there were many types of people who came through the doors. And I learned from all the people who chose to stay and hang around, you see. And some of the more… unsavory types, if you will, taught me a few essentials, such as how to pickpocket items."

There was a moment of stunned silence before Sergeant Collins said, "Do you mean to tell me you lifted a phone off of one of them?"

Jewel smiled. "Absolutely. I'm very good at it, you know. Plus I saw him enter his code, so I knew how to unlock the thing." The sergeant glowered at her, and she quickly added, "I only do it when absolutely necessary, such as recently. Anyway, one of them would come in to check on me or give me some horrible gloppy kind of food and I would snatch the phone and make a call." She stopped and shivered. "I thought they were going to hurt me. The first time the police showed up, that woman-named-after-a-city ran into the room and found the phone I'd used. She gagged me, shoved me in a closet. I tried to make as much noise as I could but nobody heard me."

Jewel shifted in her seat, and Angela said, "Are you okay to continue? Do you need anything?"

Jewel smiled at her. "No, I have my tea, thank you, and cinnamon rolls are baking in the oven so we can have a snack in a moment." The enticing aroma of yeast and cinnamon had filled the room, giving it a cozy feeling despite the crime they were discussing.

Sergeant Collins looked down at his phone. "I believe the two of them, Darren and Phoenix, kept the deputies outside every time they showed up at the house. That's what the report says. He stayed outside with the deputies then the 'grandmother' came banging out with a cane and they talked. According to the reports, they always talked outside. Except the last time you two were here." He nodded at Angela and Noah. "Nice work."

Angela's chest tightened as she tried to tamp down her anger. Why were people so horrible to each other? And at Christmas?

"They started to expect that I would get their phone, so they stopped carrying it into the room with them," Jewel said. "I think that last time was a fluke, and they forgot. As soon as I made the call, Darren came and snatched the phone right out of my hand and tied me up immediately. They weren't going to let me go free after that. That's why tonight I had to get your attention by banging the chair on the floor."

Noah cleared his throat. "Ms. Winters, I am so sorry. We honestly did not think there was a problem out here. They had us convinced that you were… that you had dementia."

Jewel took a sip of her hot tea, looking like she was lost in thought. "Yes, but I knew someone would eventually miss me. They were very clever, taking over my social media and telling everyone I was going on vacation and wouldn't be online for a while. I know they really wanted my monthly checks and a free place to stay, but hopefully they will have a long time in prison to think about the error of their ways."

A timer dinged on the oven, and Jewel stood, put on an oven mitt, and pulled a tray out. "I'll just let these cool before we put the icing on." From the look on Noah's face, Angela guessed he didn't care if there was icing or not. The smell was heavenly, and it was getting late.

"I have one more question," Angela said softly. "When I was in your backyard tonight, it looked like you were signaling with a mirror or something. What was that?"

Jewel gave her a broad smile. "Angela, right?" Angela nodded. "You are indeed my Angel. A regular Christmas Angel who came to rescue me. Thank you, my dear." Her eyes filled for a moment and she stopped to collect herself before continuing. "What you saw was not a mirror but my watch." She stretched her left arm out for them to see a watch on her wrist, a black leather band with the watch set in a silver case, the numbers clearly visible as Roman numerals. She pointed to the face of the watch. "This is, in fact, crystal, and I've been playing with trying to get it to reflect off the light bulb from the lamp in the room. My hands were tied in front of me, so I was able to angle my wrist with the light. I knew you were coming when you flashed your light into my room. I'm so glad it worked."

Angela let out a breath she hadn't realized she'd been holding. "Me too."

Merry Christmas Baby by Etta James played softly in the background, and the succulent smell of sauteed garlic and onion wafted through the air. Soft lights twinkled everywhere, a sign of hope in the darkness. Angela and her family raised a glass to toast the evening.

Jewel began. "I would like to thank you all for taking me in at the last minute. My original plans to be on a beach during the holiday season seem so far away right now, but I am especially grateful to be home for Christmas this year… and safe. I've known some of you from my days at The Wharf…" She glanced at Angela's parents. "But I am truly looking forward to remaining friends with the rest of you for a very, very long time." She raised her glass higher and aimed a warm smile at Angela. "And special thanks to my angel."

Angela was grateful for everyone at the table, and she was thankful her role in law enforcement meant she'd been able to help someone. She liked Jewel and knew she'd made a friend for life. "To family and friends, old and new. May we all find a way to take care of each other, no matter what we encounter along the way."

Narielle Living is the president and founder of Blue Fortune Enterprises, a publishing company who believes that books have the power to change lives. She is also the managing editor for the Williamsburg, Virginia magazine *Next Door Neighbors* and has written hundreds of do-it-yourself articles for online magazines.

Narielle is the author of the mysteries *Signs of the South*, *Revenge of the Past*, *Christmas in Virginia*, *Madness in Brewster Square*, and *Birding in Brewster Square*, and she co-authored *Chesapeake Bay Karma—The Amulet*. In addition, her fiction appears in the Chesapeake Bay Writers' first anthology, *Harboring Secrets*. She edits both fiction and nonfiction and loves helping other writers achieve their goals. Narielle is currently working on her next books, which include the next mystery in the Brewster Square series and a memoir about adoption.

For more information about Narielle or her books, you can find her at blue-fortune.com.

"If more of us valued food and cheer and song above hoarded gold, it would be a merrier world."

J.R.R. Tolkien, *The Hobbit*

Snowflakes

by Patti Gaustad Procopi

Joey, Tommy, and Katie did not have happy childhoods. Their mother was a habitual drug user and a drunk. Katie sometimes wondered why her mother had even had children when, for the most part, she was not interested in them. After having three children almost three years in a row, her mother was finally convinced by a social worker to have her tubes tied. The social worker did not make the extra effort to check on the children she currently had.

Katie, the oldest, did her best to take care of her younger brothers but at the age of six, there was only so much she could do. Their mother did not spend money on food or clothes, so Katie developed a system of hoarding food from the kindergarten she attended to bring back to the house later. Joey and Tommy were too young for school and didn't get the advantage of the free lunch program or the scrutiny of teachers and other staff.

The men that their mother brought home sometimes scared Katie. They were often drunk and brutal and many nights as the children hid in bed huddled together, they heard violent altercations from their mother's bedroom. The men came and went on an almost a daily basis, though occasionally one would stick around for as long as a week. Katie kept her brothers quiet and out of sight as much as possible.

Doug was the only exception to their mother's usual men. First because he stayed for months and secondly because he really seemed to love their mother and wanted to help her. He was the first of the men who actually spoke to Katie and her brothers. He seemed genuinely interested in the children and their well-being.

"Your mom is a good person, deep down," he often told them. "She's just had a hard life."

He tried to get their mother to care about them as well. Often he would arrive at the apartment with bags of groceries and make dinner for the children. "Kids need food. They aren't air plants," he said to their mother with concern. Their mother's only response to this was to shrug and light a cigarette while popping open another beer.

Katie had learned early on not to rely on adults. Especially her mother but also the other adults who drifted in and out of their lives. Doug was the first person she began to trust and believe in. She never understood why he stayed with her mother, who was not a very pleasant person, but Katie was glad he was there.

One weekend, Doug showed up with coats and sweaters for all the children. "Do you realize that it's winter outside? The children can't go around in t-shirts in this weather." He only got the usual shrug from their mother.

The next weekend Doug announced they should go out and find a Christmas tree to decorate. "Christmas is almost here. We need to get a tree and hang up our stockings for Santa." Katie and her brothers stared at him. They had never had a tree or decorated for Christmas. Katie had heard about Santa and Christmas from some of the kids at school, who talked endlessly about what they hoped to get for Christmas. Once she'd asked her mother about Santa and the presents he brought. Her mother sneered at her. "Grow up. Santa is just BS. Ain't nobody flying around giving kids presents, and I ain't got no money to buy you guys nuthin'. You're lucky you ain't out on the streets." Katie thought it might not be any worse to live on the streets than in their stinky, filthy apartment.

When Doug found out the kids had never had a Christmas tree, he was shocked. "Didn't you have a family when you were a kid? Didn't you have a Christmas tree? And decorations?"

Their mother rolled her eyes. "Right. I lived in a beautiful house with all those things." Her lips twisted into a grimace. "Oh wait. No. I lived with my drunk father, who beat me until I escaped when I was fourteen. So, I ain't interested in fairy tales."

Doug was not discouraged. He brought a tiny artificial tree to the apartment and helped the kids cut out paper garlands to hang on it. Then he said he had a special treat planned for them that weekend. He arrived on Saturday and told them to bundle up. Their mom sat curled on the couch, a blanket wrapped around her. "Have fun."

"Aren't you coming?" Doug asked.

"Hell no. Too cold. I'm not feeling well." She said and pulled the blanket tighter.

Katie could tell Doug was angry, but he was not giving up. "Let's go, kids," he said enthusiastically. They marched out of the apartment, down the stairs, and into his car. He drove to an area of Williamsburg that Katie didn't recognize. Even though she had lived her whole life in the town, her mother never took them out so all Katie knew was their apartment block and school. Doug parked the car. "We'll have to walk a bit. But it's not too cold."

As they walked, Doug told them stories about how people lived in the old days. He called it "colonial' times". He explained these people enjoyed the holidays and loved to decorate and celebrate. They finally arrived at a wide street that was not paved like the streets Katie knew but seemed to be made up of small blocks of stones. People on the street wore strange clothes. Women in hats and long dresses and men in short pants with long socks and funny three-cornered hats, not ball caps. Some stood around in groups, singing. The houses were covered with tree branches, fruit, feathers, and ribbons. Doug would point out some of the more elaborate decorations and ask Katie if she thought they were pretty. Katie thought they were strange but she liked them, so she nodded enthusiastically at Doug.

As the sun began to sink low in the sky, bundles of wood set in baskets on tall metal poles were lit. It added warmth and light to the streets. The old city was even more beautiful in the evening. Doug had bought them apple cider and gingerbread cookies. Katie had never had either before and she thought they were wonderful. The cider was warm and the cookies had a spicy taste. Her brothers seemed to like them as well and gobbled up every bite.

They followed a crowd of people to a big open area where a huge evergreen tree was positioned. A man stood by a microphone and welcomed everyone and then the tree lit up with thousands of lights. People were all singing songs they seemed to know without having to look at words on paper. It was the most fabulous thing she had ever experienced. As they stared up at the tree, it started to snow. Doug laughed. "Stick your tongue out and catch the snowflakes." Katie tried and smiled when she caught one and it melted on her tongue. She grinned up at Doug.

"When I was a kid, my parents brought the whole family here every year and we would walk around and see all the decorations. But the highlight was always the tree," Doug said to her as they watched the snow drift down. Katie knew she would come back every year to see the tree with her brothers, just like Doug's family had done.

Joey was half asleep when Doug picked him up to carry back to the car. "Keep an eye on Tommy, Katie. We have to go now." Doug held Katie's hand and Katie held Tommy's as they walked. Even though the drive home wasn't long, they all fell asleep. Doug gently shook Katie awake. "We're back home. Need to get upstairs and get you three in bed."

They walked in the door and Katie was immediately struck by the smell. Doug set Joey down and rushed into the living room. Katie herded her brothers into their room and told them to go to sleep. She then followed Doug into the living room. She saw Doug on his knees, pushing on her mother's chest. He yelled into his phone at the same time. Her mother was covered in vomit which permeated the room with a horrible odor.

Katie wasn't sure how much time had passed but suddenly the apartment was filled with people while flashing lights from the outside flicked across the ceiling. Uniformed men placed her mother on a stretcher and began to take her out of the door. Doug saw Katie standing there and said, "Katie. Go to bed. It's okay. Your mother will be fine." Katie wasn't sure she believed him but she went and snuggled in bed with her brothers. A short time later, she heard knocking on the door and the murmur of voices. Doug was still there, but she wasn't sure who the other voices belonged to.

The door creaked open, and a woman's voice said, "Katie?"

"Yes." Katie sat up.

"Hi there. My name is Barbara. I'm from child protective services." She walked into the room and sat on the edge of the bed. "Your mother has been taken to the hospital. I'm not sure when she might be coming home, but it won't be tonight and you three can't stay here alone so I'm going to take you with me to a safe place for the night or maybe a few nights."

Katie didn't understand. She didn't want to go with this strange woman. She didn't understand who this person was or where she wanted to take them. "Can't we stay here with Doug until Mom comes home?"

"No honey. Doug is not your father or a relative."

Doug suddenly appeared in the doorway. "Don't worry, sweetie. It will be okay. It will just be for a night or two and then we'll all be back here in time to celebrate Christmas."

Barbara turned the light on and helped Katie pack up clothes. Everything for the three of them fit in one garbage bag. "Do you have any special things you want to take? A stuffed animal or a blanket? Something to make you feel like home?" Katie shook her head slowly. She didn't want to tell this woman that they had nothing like that.

Doug jumped in. "Santa was going to bring all that on Christmas. Right Katie?"

Katie barely nodded as she stared down at the floor. She didn't want to look at this woman. She wanted Doug to stop her from taking them away. Even though their apartment was not nice, it was their home. Barbara took the bag of clothes from Katie. Doug picked up Joey and Tommy, who were both still asleep, and he and Katie followed Barbara out of the apartment and down the stairs. The children were loaded into a van.

Before Barbara shut the door, Doug asked her if he could have a moment to talk to Katie. She nodded. "But be quick. We have to be on the way."

Doug bent down. "Katie. Don't worry. It will be all right." He reached out and squeezed her hand. "You have to be brave for Joey and Tommy." A tear slipped down her cheek. "None of that." Doug smiled. "You're the big sister."

He reached into his pocket and pulled out a small box. "This was going to be for Christmas morning, but I want to give it to you now." She stared at the box. "Keep it safe." She glanced up and then stuck it in her coat pocket.

"Merry Christmas. We'll be together soon."

The van door shut. Katie watched Doug out the back window until the van turned a corner and he disappeared from sight.

They arrived at a building and the children were taken upstairs to a room with three cots. "This is just temporary," Barbara said, as if apologizing. Katie didn't tell her it was much nicer than their room at home. The boys were still sound asleep and Barbara and the driver laid them on separate cots. "You can sleep in that one." She indicated the last cot. "Don't worry about getting in your pajamas tonight. We can sort everything out in the morning."

Before Barbara left, Katie asked her where the bathroom was. Barbara pointed to a door across from the beds. "Right there. It's just a toilet and a sink. The showers are down the hall."

Katie thanked her and went into the bathroom. She turned on the light and then the faucet. She wasn't sure why, but she didn't want Barbara to hear her. Katie pulled the box out of her pocket and opened it. Inside was a silver necklace with a small snowflake pendant. The snowflake seemed to have shiny crystals on it and it twinkled in the light. It was the most beautiful thing she'd ever seen. The most beautiful thing she ever owned.

Suddenly she was startled by a knock on the door. "Are you okay, hon?" Barbara asked.

"Yes." Katie closed the box and pushed it deep into her

jacket pocket. Barabara led her to her cot and said good night before turning out the light. Katie lay in bed a long time staring at the ceiling. She kept running her fingers over the box in her pocket.

The next morning, the door opened and another woman stood there. "Good morning," she said cheerfully. "I'm sure you're all hungry. Breakfast is ready." Tommy and Joey woke up at the sound of the strange voice and started to cry. Katie rushed over to comfort them. "Oh dear," the woman said. "I didn't mean to startle you. I'm sure you'll feel better after you get some food in your bellies." After calming her brothers, Katie shoved her hand into her pocket to make sure the box was there.

The children warily followed the woman to a room down the hall. They could smell food as they got closer, and Katie realized how hungry she was. All they'd had to eat the day before was a small breakfast then cookies and cider. They never got dinner. The boys started smiling as food was set in front of them. The woman poured glasses of milk while Katie cut up Joey's toast and eggs.

The rest of the day was a blur as they were taken to see various people who poked and prodded them and asked endless questions. Katie only had one question. "Where's Doug?" After asking once, and being told Doug was not her father, she didn't speak to anyone. The children's clothes, which were old, worn, and odd sizes that barely fit, were replaced with clean clothes in the right sizes.

Katie could tell they weren't brand new but they were better than anything the siblings ever had before, besides the few things Doug bought them. They did get brand new socks and shoes.

When they were changing into their new clothes, the necklace box fell out of Katie's pocket. The woman helping them bent to pick it up. "No!" Katie screamed and snatched it from the woman's hand. Then she cringed, knowing she would be punished.

"I'm sorry, honey. Is that yours? Can I see it?"

Katie reluctantly handed the box to the woman.

"Oh, that's so pretty? Did your momma give you that?" the lady asked.

Katie thought it would be better just to nod and not mention Doug.

"Well, let's put this around your neck. Much safer that way. If you're wearing it, you won't lose it." The woman fastened the necklace around Katie's neck. "Oh, look how pretty it is." Katie looked up into the mirror. The snowflake necklace twinkled in the light.

Barbara returned at the end of the day and said they would be moving out of this building to another one with other children. "They're also waiting for their mom or dad or sometimes a new home with a relative. Unfortunately, you won't be able to stay in the same room with your brothers since the children are divided. Boys in one area and girls in the other."

Katie wasn't sure what that meant. Where were her mother and Doug? When would they go home again? Wasn't their future with their mother in their own apartment? Hopefully with Doug there too.

The next morning, the children with their new clothes were taken down the stairs and climbed into the van again. They arrived at another building and when they walked inside, Tommy and Joey were led down one hall and she was led down another. Katie fought to go with her brothers. "I have to take care of them," she screamed. "They need me."

A burly woman took Katie firmly by the hand and pulled her down the hall to the girl's wing. "They'll be fine. They'll have toys and television and good food."

Katie was brought into a room with several bunk beds. The other girls in there looked as lost and scared as Katie felt. She was shown to her bunk, and she climbed in, holding on to her bag of clothes. The woman said in a kinder voice, "Barbara will be back tomorrow morning to tell you what has been decided about your immediate future."

"Who decides?" Katie managed to say.

"A judge who has your best interests at heart." Katie wanted to ask how a man she'd never met could know what was best for her and her brothers. Maybe he would send her back home. To her apartment with her mother and Doug. Katie pulled the blanket over her head and turned her back to the room.

The next morning, she was taken to an office in another part of the building. She had seen her brothers at breakfast. They appeared to be happy and unconcerned that they were no longer at home with their mother.

Barbara was sitting on a couch in the office. She smiled at Katie and patted the couch to indicate Katie should sit with her. Katie sat down warily. "I have to talk to you about your mother." Katie winced. "She is very ill. Currently she's still in the hospital. The doctors don't think she'll be able to get out soon and come back to your apartment and take care of you." Barbara paused, waiting for Katie to respond.

Katie said nothing.

"We have to find someplace else for you and your brothers to live until she gets better," Barbara said. "Do you understand?"

She understood but wondered why they couldn't just live with Doug until their mom came home. "Doug?" She finally managed to say.

"I'm afraid, as I've said before, Doug is not a relative so we can't let him take care of you." Barbara patted Katie's hand. "But don't worry, we'll find you and your brothers a good place to live."

A day later, Tommy and Joey were taken away to a foster home. Katie didn't even get to say goodbye. They left immediately after breakfast. Barbara came to her room to tell her. "I know it's hard but your brothers are going to a great home. They'll stay together. Unfortunately, we couldn't find a place for all three of you."

Katie was taken to a different foster home a few days later. She was overwhelmed. It was noisy and chaotic with lots of children. She missed her brothers. She missed Doug. The foster family took in many children. There was a constant change of inhabitants as children left for various reasons, only to be replaced with new faces.

In the twelve years she spent in foster care, Katie moved four times to different homes. She never knew why she was moved but there was no point in asking questions. Where she lived made no difference to her. She had enough to eat, clothes to wear, and a roof over her head.

At some point she learned that her brothers had been adopted a year after they went into foster care. Thankfully they were still together. Two cute cuddly little boys were easier to adopt out than a withdrawn, introverted girl who rarely spoke or smiled. One of the other foster kids told her that if her brothers were adopted, that meant her mother was either dead or had signed over her parental rights. She said this with malicious glee, as if she wanted to hurt Katie. But Katie didn't care. She never wanted to see her mother again.

Over time, Katie began to bury her past in some part of her mind. Her mother. The accident. The filthy apartment. She even forgot her brothers. The past was too painful. The present was endurable. The future unknown. The one constant in her life as she moved from place to place was the snowflake necklace. Katie didn't remember where she got it from, just that she'd always had it and when she touched it, she was oddly comforted.

At eighteen, Katie aged out of foster care. She found herself on the street with all her possessions in a suitcase she had acquired at some time over the years of moving from home to home. She found a room to rent and a job. One night as she was getting ready to leave work, she heard the other employees mention that the tree lighting was being held that evening. Something deep in her memory began to stir. A warm remembrance of a happy time. She had buried all the thoughts of her former life before she'd gone into foster care. Christmas had always annoyed her. Just a bunch of BS and lies, she thought, though she didn't know where she got that idea from.

One of her colleagues noticed the look on her face. "Have you ever been to the colonial area and seen the tree lighting?" Katie shook her head. "Come along. It's so much fun and really beautiful." Katie almost declined but something was tugging at her, encouraging her to go along.

"Okay," she said quietly. They all drove together and parked. "It's a bit of a walk but it's a nice night. Not too cold," one of her co-workers said. A walk. In the cold. They stopped at a booth and bought hot cider and gingerbread cookies. "These are the best," someone said. Katie took a sip of the cider and a bite of her cookie, and a memory struggled to come to the surface. Emotion overwhelmed her. It seemed to be a happy memory. She had so few of those. None actually. "Come on. We're going to be late." Someone laughed and tugged at her hand and smiled at her.

Someone holding her hand and smiling. The taste of the cider and cookie. They passed old houses decorated with branches, fruit, feathers, and ribbons. Katie stared in amazement. She'd been here before, and she'd been happy. The hand holding hers was suddenly the hand of her little brother... Tommy? She'd tried not to think about her little brothers over the years. It was too painful. Now she wondered about them. She squeezed the hand holding hers and felt a squeeze back.

They arrived in front of the tree. Someone was giving a speech welcoming them all to the annual event. A warm, welcoming voice. She remembered a kind voice from years ago. Instinctively, she reached up and fingered the small pendant on the chain around her neck. Once it had glittered but time and Katie had worn off the sparkles.

Suddenly a hundred, maybe a thousand lights erupted in bright color over the huge tree. Katie smiled. A genuine smile for the first time in years. It began to snow and she looked up and put her tongue out and caught a snowflake.

Merry Christmas, she thought.

Patti Gaustad Procopi is a former army brat who lived all over the world before settling in Gloucester, Virginia, with her husband Greg. They raised three daughters and numerous cats and dogs. Patti worked at two area history museums for thirty-two years. After retiring she finally had the time to do the thing she always wanted to do: write! She always loved reading and at each army post, and the library was the first place she'd seek out.

Patti's writing is about emotional connections, friendship and family. She was thrilled when her first novel, *Please… Tell Me More*, was published in 2020 by Blue Fortune Enterprises, LLC. Her second novel, *I'll Get By*, came out in 2022 and her third, *Stop Talking*, was released in late 2023. She's currently working on her first mystery.

Patti has had stories printed in literary journals and anthologies and one was read on a podcast. She's given talks at area libraries and writing symposiums about how to tell your story.

When not writing, Patti enjoys photographing birds on her creek. She also enjoys gardening, yoga, and researching her family on Ancestry. There are some stories there yet to be told. She and Greg love traveling and are slowly ticking off their bucket list.

You can find Patti's book on Barnes & Noble, Amazon, or wherever books are sold. And you can contact Patti on her website, pattiproauthor.com, or email patti.pro@cox.net or on Facebook.

"I will honour Christmas in my heart,
and try to keep it all the year."
Charles Dickens, *A Christmas Carol*

The Greatest Gift

by Bradley Harper

The people waiting to see Santa snaked around the building, and Santa Mark found his third day on the job more of an assembly line for commercial enterprise than making magic. By now, he could guess with about ninety percent accuracy what toys the boys (trucks, dinosaurs, and Pokémon Trading Cards) and girls (Barbie with her vast collection of homes and accessories, and occasional dinosaurs) would ask for, indicative of the power of modern advertising.

He was ninety minutes into his two-hour shift at the park when his elf had the next group wait while she came up to him. Santa Mark hated anything that slowed the process down, so he raised an eyebrow as she approached.

"I'm sorry, Santa," Twinkles the Elf said, "but the next three children were orphaned a year ago."

"And?"

Twinkles swallowed before answering. "The foster parents have just been approved to adopt all three of them so they can grow up together."

"That's nice," he said, grudgingly. "So?"

She blushed. "The parents want you to tell them."

Then, before Santa Mark had a chance to think, there they were, a girl around twelve and two boys, roughly ten and eight. The girl was playing it cool for her younger brothers, while the ten-year-old was clearly on the fence, finding the myth of Santa increasingly hard to swallow but afraid to blow his chances in case he was wrong.

The eight-year-old's brown eyes were large and shiny. A true believer.

Mark's mind raced through and discarded a dozen greetings in a half-second before falling back on the tried and true, "Hello, and what would you like for Christmas?"

Each child dutifully recited their short list, but Santa Mark was oblivious to anything they said as he panicked, wondering how he could possibly share this good news with his three earnest petitioners.

The eight-year-old was last, and after Santa Mark promised he would "look into it," he stared at the three and prayed for inspiration.

"Keep it simple," a voice said within, so he did.

"Those are all great ideas, but I have something for you today."

"What's that, Santa?" the girl asked, apparently the spokesperson for the group.

Santa Mark took a deep breath and said, "A family."

The three looked puzzled. "You are living with a wonderful couple right now, correct?"

They nodded, and he continued. "This couple is going to adopt you. All of you. Everyone gets to live in the same house. To grow up together."

They were silent, staring at Santa as though he'd started speaking Greek. Then the oldest shuddered as her two younger brothers came up to her, one under each arm. Still, they said nothing.

"Did you understand what I said?" Santa asked.

She nodded, the boys nodded, then they began to cry with joy. There wasn't a dry eye in Santa's throne room. Even the photographer broke down.

As for Santa? Well, perhaps a bit of chimney ash had gotten into his eyes, too.

After many photos, the three children were led away by their new parents, and Santa Mark was able to breathe again.

He realized how lucky he was to occupy that seat. He had been handed the trust and love of thousands of children whose names he would never recall, though his picture beside them might hang on a wall for decades to come.

He also understood the true heroes of the day were the parents who'd entrusted him to create that magical moment—when three plus two became one. One family.

At that moment, Santa Mark retired from being a pitchman for toys and became a confidante to children, ready to listen to their dreams and, if not grant them, honor them all.

If that's not magic, what is?

Bradley Harper is a retired US Army physician who began writing after retirement. During his time serving in Colombia with US Special Forces, the FARC (the Revolutionary Armed Forces of Colombia) placed a $1.5 million bounty for his capture. (Offer no longer valid.)

Dr. Harper's debut novel, *A Knife in the Fog*, was a 2019 Edgars Finalist for Best First Novel by an American. The book won Killer Nashville's Silver Falchion award as Best Mystery, and the audiobook won Audiofile Magazine's Earphone award in the Mystery category. The book has been translated into Japanese and German and is a Recommended Read by the Arthur Conan Doyle estate.

The sequel, *Queen's Gambit*, won the 2020 Silver Falchion as Best Suspense and Book of the Year. His recently produced short animation, *Dark Tryst*, has won multiple awards across Europe. His poetry and essays have been published in various magazines. He recently co-wrote a memoir by Leslie Lautenslager, *My Time with Colin Powell*, about her twenty-five years as GEN Powell's personal assistant, and his detective story, *Reflections in a Dragon's Eye*, is a 2024 Finalist for the Silver Falchion Award.

Doctor Harper recently received his master's degree in creative writing from Napier University in Edinburgh. While residing in the UK, he was voted a Fellow of the Royal Scottish Society for the Arts after his presentation, "Sherlock Holmes as Science Fiction," detailing how Doyle's character inspired the world's first crime lab.

You can follow him on Facebook at Bradley Harper-Author, and on X (Twitter) @BHarperAuthor.

His website is http://www.BHarperAuthor.Com

The Homecoming

by Kathy Kasunich

The morning haze nearly vanished as my companion, Justin, and I drive up the winding gravel road. The sound of crunching stones under the tires echoed in the tranquil air as we parked beside the cozy, weathered cabin. "Justin", my pops' 1995 Ford Taurus station wagon, had transported us to our beach getaway until Mama passed away. After cancer consumed Mama, Pops parked the car in the garage and never drove it again. It felt good to see Justin in his rightful place outside the family bungalow.

I remember the day Pops pulled into the driveway, honking the horn and calling us to check out the new car.

My brothers and I argued for hours about what to name it. I'm not sure how the tradition started, but every time a new vehicle graced our front yard, it had to be christened. Being the youngest and the only girl, I guilted them into letting me title the car. I did what any young girl in the '90s would do. I dubbed the car after my favorite singer, Justin Timberlake from NSYNC. Even though I should probably rename it now that I'm married, driving this old clunker with a different moniker wouldn't be the same. The name Justin evokes the essence of an old friend who witnessed my childhood and reminds me of those times.

A couple of years ago, when the doctor told Pops he shouldn't drive anymore, he signed the relic over to me. I suspected my brothers were upset that I acquired our "old friend." I never asked why he did it. Perhaps it was because I called him daily and often made the journey from North Carolina to spend a weekend with him. Or he felt I was the only one who still needed him. What's done is done—not my fault.

Six months have slipped by since we buried Pops. The lawyer sorted through all his affairs, and the house and his other car found new owners. The debts have been settled, and Pops' cherished belongings were either passed down to one of the kids or grandkids or donated to Goodwill. Now, all that needed attention was the family cabin.

It's hard to believe we once loved this place and boasted to our friends about our beach house, despite it not actually being on the beach. Now, the shutters hung sideways, one seemingly whisked away by the wind. The paint—dry, cracked, and discolored—evoked memories of my granny's skin before she passed. A small garden of tree saplings, flowers, and weeds sprouted from the gutters. The rusted outdoor furniture and screen door, riddled with holes and adorned with feathers and leaves, gave the cabin an eerie look. For a second, my eyes scanned the perimeter for a man with a chainsaw and mask. Mama would have been heartbroken to see this place in such ruins. I shuddered to think what the inside might look like.

The door creaked as I pushed it open, causing my spine to tingle. "Aaaaahh!" I screamed and jumped as something scampered over my feet. Dust danced in the streams of light peeking through the blinds. The air hung heavy with the damp, musty smell of a cave, intensified by the mold and the unmistakable scent of animal droppings. There was no electricity, no water, and a layer of dust had settled over every surface, enough filth to fill several vacuum cleaners.

I'm not sure what Pops was thinking when he stipulated in his will that we all needed to spend a week at the old cabin before the attorney released the money from his estate. This was the first time we would be at the beach house since Mama passed. Pops knew that for the last decade, our already frayed relationship continued to unravel. Perhaps he wanted to look down from heaven and see us together once more, talking and reconnecting instead of being distant. *Or he's enjoying a laugh by inflicting one more punishment on us*, I thought. *Pops is wielding the upper hand and having the last word, as usual.*

Although the place was in shambles, as I cast the lantern light around the room, my mind wandered to better days. In an instant, a flood of recollections washed over me with the force of Niagara Falls. Images played in my mind like an old movie. Mama in the rocking chair, knitting and laughing at Pops' corny jokes. Billy, Joe, Bobby, and I playing Monopoly on the floor. Small puddles of water and sand scattered over the floor as we raced in from the beach. In the kitchen, fish freshly caught from the Chesapeake Bay frying in the pan, and me helping Mama make corn muffins. Singing, card games, and pillow fights. Crab traps, fishing gear, and wet towels piled high in the corner. Then it's December, and the beach-themed tree twinkled while the fireplace glowed, ready for the skewers of marshmallows, as the old stereo played Christmas tunes. By the time another car rumbled over the rocks, I had exhausted two boxes of Kleenex and a roll of toilet paper.

Bob parked on the overgrown grass, the tires sinking into the soft earth. My brothers traipsed out, looking weary as they dragged their gear from the car.

I stepped onto the front porch. "What took y'all so

long? Y'all said you'd be here by sunrise."

"You realize I made two stops along the way to pick these guys up?" Bob said in defense.

"Yeah, but you were an hour late picking me up," Joe said.

"That's not my fault. You know I-95 sucks any time of day. Besides, after we picked up Billy, we backtracked fifteen miles because he forgot the propane tank."

"That's because you were yelling at me to hurry up and get in. We wasted more time eating at the diner because Joe insisted on getting food so he could take his pills."

I couldn't believe they hadn't even stepped foot in the cabin, and they were already complaining. "Stop your bickering already! Get over here and help me carry these boxes inside. And if Pops were here, he'd say let's get this place cleaned up right quick."

Billy nodded at his brother. "Hey Bob, are you going to help clean or are you waiting for your maids to show up?"

Bob put up his fist. "I oughta…"

I stomped my foot and screamed, "For Pete's sake, give it up! We've got a ton of work to do. The sooner we knock it out, the sooner we can each do our thing here, and honor Pop's last wish. Go pick a room and stay in your own corner and we'll get it done."

Billy shot a piercing look at Bob, snatched a bucket and broom, and stormed off toward the back bedroom.

Bob muttered under his breath while grabbing rags and

a garbage bag, his brow furrowed and his steps resolute.

Joe made a swift dash for the bathroom and slammed the door behind him, causing the living room vintage chandelier to sway. *I can't believe it didn't crash to the floor*, I thought.

As for the kitchen, everyone seemed to assume it was my domain since I'm a woman. What happened to equality?

Several hours later, the cabin began to look habitable, a far cry from the eerie haunt I first entered. Tired and hungry, we unanimously agreed to tackle the finer details over the coming days.

"I guess we need to decide what we're going to do about sleeping arrangements," Bob said.

I had been considering this dilemma before I left home. "I didn't want to sleep in any of the beds because I knew they'd be full of dust, so I brought some sleeping bags and blankets if you want them. I say we set up the sleeping bags in front of the fireplace. It's the only room that has heat and light from the fire."

"Do you think we can survive being in the same room all night?" Joe asked.

"All I know is if anybody talks in their sleep or snores, I'm kicking you out," Bob threatened.

"The hell you will. I'll punch your lights out if you try," Billy countered.

Feeling the need to play referee, I stood between the

boys, extending my arms to block any punches. "Okay, okay. That's enough. Why is everything a brouhaha? For Mama and Pops' sake, let's try to get along. When we were kids, we loved having a sleepover in front of the fire. We'd sneak a few sips of Pops' whiskey, tell ghost stories, and stay up until the sun rose. We always had a good time."

"Bets, we're not kids anymore. Things have changed," Bob said.

"Have they? I think I'm still the same person I was before, only older and wiser."

"Maybe you are, Bets. But I've changed. I don't have time for nostalgia or childish activities. Except for the swigs of whiskey. I should be at work—I've got a lot of responsibility and a lot on my mind. I just hope my staff can handle my clients," Bob said with a sigh.

"Oh, that's right, you're Mr. Big Shot," Billy interjected.

"Are you jealous because you've been in the same dead-end job for years?" Bob snapped.

"If you'd ever call me, you'd realize I got a new job as regional manager three years ago," Billy said.

"Seriously, you guys can't let it go for a few days?"

"Listen, Betsy's right," Joe said. "This may be the last time we're all together and the final thing we have to do before we move on. I say we try our best to get along and treat it like a week of vacation or reconnection. This week could be a chance for us to catch up on each other's lives."

"Joe, don't tell me you're buying into this crap," Bob

interjected sharply. "Acting like we're some tight-knit family."

"I'm just tired of all the fighting, especially at Christmas." Joe countered, a hint of nostalgia in his voice. "And yes, we were close. Being here, I really miss Ma and Pops." Joe shook his head, turned toward the door, and sighed, "Anyway, whether we bunk together or not, we're gonna need wood. Anyone want to help me?"

"You can get the wood. I'm going to the beach to get some fresh air." Bob grabbed his coat and phone.

"I'm going down to the store to get a pack of smokes," Billy said.

Exasperated by the situation, I threw my arms in the air, plopped onto the overstuffed chair, and talked to the picture of Ma and Pops, who were sitting in the boat smiling. "I really thought this last time here would be different. I can't believe my memories of this place are going to be tainted by this final visit. I want us to get along, but I don't know what to do."

I hugged the frame before placing it back on the end table. "I wish you were here. You'd know what to do."

As I sat in the silent, cold room, I reflected on the task Pops initiated for us. I knew my brothers were busy living their lives, but my life was full of demanding tasks too. Cleaning this cabin a couple of weeks before Christmas was the last thing I needed to be doing. But I also wanted to move on and cross this task off my to-do list so I could enjoy Christmas with my family. If only they knew how much I missed all of us together. Sure, we used to fight like all siblings do—arguing, crying, and screaming—but somehow, within an hour, we'd forget why we were mad. Bob was right; we weren't kids anymore.

The only room we needed to declutter was the attic. Even though I dreaded going up there as a kid, with its spider webs and the occasional mouse, I decided now was the time to tackle it.

I pulled down the attic steps, and decades of dust and dead bugs rained over me. I brushed the debris out of my hair and, with lantern and broom in hand, I forged into the unknown. It was filled to the rafters. In boxes faded and crumbling, I found extra kitchen supplies, worn-out toys, beach gear, and worn outdated clothes—remnants of our life at the beach packed away, preserved and forgotten. Memories engulfed my mind like waves crashing on the shore. It was hard to recall a visit to the cabin that hadn't been fun. Between our adventures and the activities Ma and Pops planned, there was never a dull moment. I wished this time machine could summon Ma and Pops to relive those days. Life here wasn't flawless, but it was uniquely us. We shared treasured traditions, tales, and precious moments, enjoying the simple pleasures of life.

After college, our careers scattered us across three states, and our lives became consumed with schedules, obligations, and deadlines. Distance and sporadic phone calls and texts hindered our relationships. Sibling rivalry and jealousy added to the mix, especially when someone got a new house, car, or promotion. Mama always had a knack for soothing tensions, especially when our green eyes appeared with envy or disappointment. If she were here now, she'd find a way to help us realize the importance of keeping the lines of communication open. This place would be infused with fun. and she'd be ecstatic to see the grandkids joining in the excitement. Pops would have loved it, too.

I rifled through the boxes, each artifact a reminder of days gone by. *These will all have to go before we sell the house,* I thought. *Letting go of this treasure chest of memories feels impossible. If we discard these boxes, are we erasing our past?*

Tears welled up in my eyes as I pushed the boxes toward the stairs. A few steps closer to abandoning the artifacts of our past life.

"Hey Betsy, you up there?" It was Joe, probably back with the wood.

I glanced down the stairs and saw Bob and Billy join Joe, squinting in my direction.

Bob asked Joe, "What's going on? You two hiding something?"

"Nothing's going on. I just got here and was wondering what Betsy was doing."

Before they started fighting again, I said, "Hey, I need help with a bunch of stuff we're going to have to weed through. Stay there. I'm going to send it down."

I passed each box to Joe, who handed it to Bob and finally to Billy, who placed them in the corner. The assembly line rolled along quickly, leaving no time for the boys to make any derogatory remarks.

"What is all this stuff? Billy asked.

To others, the reply might have been more specific. I sighed and said, "Our life!"

Bob snorted. "It's going to take us all week to get through this junk."

There were still some piles on the other side of the attic. "Maybe longer," I said. "There's more. Wait a minute while I get it."

In the corner, I peeked underneath a stack of blankets, and my breath caught in my throat. Christmas presents, forgotten for decades, wrapped in faded holiday paper. The first one I retrieved was addressed to Joe from Santa. Beside it lay a slew of gifts, all bearing the unmistakable squiggly square letters of my mother's "Santa" writing. Despite us being older, Mama still held onto the treasured tradition of Santa. Mama and Pops adored Christmas, infusing it with magic and warmth. I remembered the year Mama sprinkled fake snow all over the roof, leaving sleigh prints in the snow. The following year, "Santa's" boot print outlined in ashes adorned the wooden floor by the fireplace. The Peter Pan syndrome was alive and well in their world during December, never breaking character in their belief in Santa and their commitment to making it the most magical time.

Christmas wasn't just a day; it was a month-long celebration. Right after Thanksgiving, we'd decorate every inch of the house. The season was filled with Christmas shopping, baking, watching the Santa Parade down Main Street and classic Christmas movies. The week before Christmas, we packed the car to the brim and drove to our house by the beach. After we cut down a tree from our property, we'd gather seashells and whatever we could find to decorate the tree. As we strung popcorn (and ate some, too), we added homemade ornaments crafted from construction paper, twigs, and cotton balls. To steal a sentiment from a song, it was the most wonderful time of the year.

"What's taking so long?" Joe called with impatience.

"Hold your horses. I'm coming. You're not going to believe what I found." I passed two boxes to Joe. "Here, take these."

"Oh my God, are these old Christmas presents?" Joe exclaimed.

"Wow, we have a genius in our midst," Bob said. "How'd you figure that out so quickly?"

Joe's voice rose. "Quit being a smart ass. It was a rhetorical question. If you know what that means?" He glanced at the gifts. "I just can't believe these presents are here. Ma must have bought and wrapped them before she passed away, and Pops never came back to get them."

As I handed down another piece from the past, I said, "These gifts are Ma's last gesture of love."

Bob hung his head and in a hushed voice said, "It feels like she's here."

"If only that were true," Billy said.

I brought the last present with me as I descended the attic stairs and placed it with the rest.

"What should we do?" Joe asked. "Do we open them?"

We stood in silence, staring at the forgotten gifts, as if we had just uncovered the Holy Grail.

Bob finally broke the silence. "Seeing all these boxes with Ma's writing is bringing back so many emotions and memories I buried a long time ago because it hurt to remember." His voice wavered and I saw tears forming in his eyes. "It's unsettling, like reopening a door I thought I'd closed for good."

Billy put his arm around Bob. "I know what you mean."

Joe, looking faint, walked over and dropped onto the couch. "This is a little overwhelming. I didn't expect to find anything like this."

The sun disappeared and the house grew dark. No one seemed to mind, and we reflected on the discovery. Soon, my happiness and grief poured from me and my sobbing echoed off the walls. I needed to commemorate this moment and translate my feelings into something meaningful. I took a deep breath to calm myself and blurted, "I know this is a crazy idea, but in the spirit of Ma and Pops, what if we try to have one more Christmas like we used to? We could find a small tree to cut down and decorate it with some oyster shells and popcorn garland."

Without hesitation Bob said, "When I was cleaning, I came across some old records. If the player still works, we can listen to music."

"We don't have any electricity," Joe reminded him.

Billy said, "There's an old radio in the bedroom. We can find a station that plays Christmas music. All we need are batteries. Did you bring any, Bets?"

I rustled through the box of supplies. "There are batteries in these extra flashlights. That should work."

"I'll see if I can catch some crabs and catfish in the morning, and we can have crab meat and eggs for breakfast and catfish and grits for dinner like the old days," Joe said.

Billy smiled like an eager child. "And when it gets dark, we can open the presents."

In a magical minute, the atmosphere transformed from gloom and tension to anticipation and excitement. "Well, I'll be. The Christmas spirit has woken up and found you all. Or else Mama and Pops mustered up a Christmas miracle," I said.

The next day went as planned. The tree, decorations, breakfast, and dinner were perfect. When we sat around the fire to open the presents, we were no longer estranged siblings but fun-loving kids, basking in the joy of the

Christmas season. We laughed, joked, and ate s'mores as we unwrapped the gifts. Bob almost cried when he unwrapped the baseball mitt he had begged for. Joe actually jumped up with excitement when he opened the Bon Jovi album and exclaimed, "I still love this group!" Billy invited us to play his game of Trivial Pursuit. When I opened the box to find an artist Barbie, tears streamed down my face. How did Ma know I would be a graphic artist when I grew up? I wanted to run to her and hug her and tell her about my life since she left us.

We unwrapped gift after gift, each one brimming with nostalgia. As the night progressed, the tension between us slowly dissolved. Laughter replaced arguments, and soon we were backslapping and finding common ground. By the time we finished opening our treasures, playing a game of Trivial Pursuit, and reminiscing about everything, the sun's rays peeped through the curtains.

"Morning already?" Joe said. "I can hardly believe it."

Bob yawned. "The time did fly. You know, I came here with a piss-poor attitude and couldn't wait for this week to be over, but now I wish it wouldn't end."

"Bob, I can't believe you softened up. What happened?" Billy asked.

"I don't know. I've done a lot of contemplating since I've been here. I have a great job and I love it, but I think I work too much and don't spend enough time with the kids. Like Ma and Pops spent with us. You know, sometimes life just gets in the way of having a good time. These past two days have reminded me that I need to take time for family and make memories before it's too late."

"You're right," Joe said. "Life is short. Ma died young and you know..."

I thought about the cabin and their statements, and I realized the cabin held the key to keeping our memories and our relationship alive. "You know, life is short! But we can make it better. Did the will say we have to sell this place?"

"I don't know. All I know is that we couldn't sell it until we stayed here. Why?"

"If we fix this place up, it could be more than just a cabin. It could be Ma and Pops' legacy, a place where our kids can make their own memories."

"Yeah, why not?" Bob said. "I sure could use some time away from the office and get to know my kids. They could play some board games instead of those stupid video games they spend hours playing. They could even learn how to fish."

"I'd love for my kids to see this place and appreciate the pleasures of beach life," Joe said.

Billy added, "I think it's a great idea."

I smiled at the thought of us holding on to the cabin of our youth. As I glanced at the framed photo of Mama and Pops on the mantle, I felt Ma's warm embrace and Pops' hand on my shoulder. I picked up the photo and placed it on the coffee table between us. "You know, Ma and Pops might be gone, but they're still directing things. I think this was Pops' plan all along. I think he didn't want to sell Old Justin because he believed the memories might fade if he did." I paused. "And maybe he doesn't want us to sell the cabin, so we never forget how important family is and remember how much we care about each other, despite each of us going our own way. What do you say we talk to the attorney, figure out how much this will cost to make it livable, and meet back here after the holidays?"

They all agreed to the plan and shared the sentiment that this Christmas season would be one to remember. For the first time in years, we were home. What once was, would continue, as the family memories, childhood escapades, and traditions reminded us of who we are and bound us for years to come.

Kathy Kasunich, originally from Pittsburgh, Pennsylvania, now resides in Williamsburg, Virginia. Her debut novel, *Always Remembering*, is a historical fiction romance set during World War II. Released in 2022, the novel has been nominated for a medal by the Military Writers Society of America (MWSA). Kathy also enjoys writing short stories and poems and is currently working on a new novel set in 18th-century Williamsburg.

As a member of the Chesapeake Bay Writers and the Writers Guild of Virginia, Kathy remains actively engaged in the literary community. In addition to her writing, she finds inspiration through photography, nature, and music, often blending these passions to enrich her creative process. More information can be found at her website https://kathykasunich.us2.authorhomepage.com/

The Stocking

by Sonja McGiboney

When it came to weird, my grammy in Williamsburg, Virginia, wins the prize. According to Grammy, her days were numbered, so when she had to move from her large home into a tiny apartment in a retirement village, she decorated for every one of her favorite holidays and left them up year-round. She didn't want to put stuff in storage. When I asked her about maybe cleaning some of it up, she always said, "Katherine, I spent all my years collecting this stuff, I want to die with all of it out to enjoy." Walking into her house was like walking into a holiday kaleidoscope.

Red hearts dotted the walls on either side of the foyer

hallway, mixed with photos of my grandpa, who had died years ago, my mom and dad, and the rest of the family.

Farther into the hallway, shamrocks and clover lined the walls. A huge leprechaun cutout hung on the hall bathroom door. Grammy said, "If I got to sit on a pot, I want it to be a lucky one." She had Dad install six floating shelves in a staggered pattern, like a zipper, on which she put statues of leprechauns, fairies, and butterflies. She even had a small pot of gold. When she first moved into the apartment and was putting up all the decorations, I asked her how much it was worth. Her answer was simple: "Oh, Katherine, my dear, it's just a pile of pyrite, or fool's gold, but the promise that you see in it is worth more than any gold you can own."

Across from the fairies, Grammy hung Mardi Gras masks. She said she got them all when she and Grandpa went to New Orleans all the time. Some of them were pretty, with gold and green sequins. Some were kind of scary, with full clown faces that didn't smile and horns sprouting at odd angles. I used to be creeped out by them and wondered why she would have such ugly masks. She said, "Life has horns, get over it." I guess I did.

The foyer opened up to a small living room. On two bookcases, on opposite sides of the entrance, bunnies and baskets of eggs lined the bottom two shelves, while fake daffodils and more bunnies sat on the top. One of my favorite figurines was a bunny in a tutu doing a pirouette.

She said she bought that when I started ballet class at age four.

The window on the left side of the room made a natural barrier between Mother's Day and July the Fourth. On the Mother's Day side were cards, some store bought but many handmade by my mom and later me. Dried up flowers wrapped in a "Happy Mother's Day" ribbon sat atop a small accent table.

The Fourth of July space (side?) had a large, framed photo of Grandpa, who had served in the Navy for thirty years, and my dad, who had been in the Army for twenty-five. A flag, neatly folded in a triangle and framed in wood and glass, hung next to my grandpa's picture. Surrounding both were a collection of little flags glued to sticks for parades.

Grammy told me a story about those flags. "When we were in France for the twenty-fifth reunion of D-day, I sat next to your grandpa in a Jeep while it slowly made its way down Le Grand Rue. French people ran up to our jeep and handed over bags of chocolates and other food items, all decorated with these little American flags. When I saw the pain mixed with thankfulness on their faces, that's when I forgave your grandpa for joining the Navy after Pearl Harbor and for all the years that he left me alone to deal with children and his mother's cancer while he went overseas fighting for other people."

The great wall in the living room, as Grammy called

it, was reserved for art. She loved bright and cheery paintings and hung all the ones that had adorned her large house on that one wall. Not a space could be seen between the frames. Even when two pictures were different sizes, she filled in the space with tiny frames of family, like the wallet-sized school pictures we sent her or family pictures she downloaded from Facebook later on.

On the tables next to the couch, the coffee table, and on her desk, a variety of knickknacks took up real estate. My one-eyed squirrel and my six-legged dog stood proudly next to some of her ceramic pumpkins, crystal dragons, and porcelain witches. Grammy loved Halloween. She said, "Growing up on the farm were some of the happiest days of my life. Especially at harvest time. We always had plenty to eat and took great care to spread our extra to our neighbors. We used to take the horse and wagon until the road was paved and the cars became dependable. But oh, a ride in the wagon in the brisk weather made you feel so alive."

In the kitchen, the chickens and cows took over. Not a holiday, she'd say, but just like one, they made her happy.

But out of all the holiday décor that took up massive space in her house, she had only one item for Christmas.

A lonely, knitted stocking with small tears near the heel hung on the five-inch end of the wall separating the kitchen from the dining room. In all the Christmases that she lived in that tiny apartment, she never put up a tree or any other ornaments.

Grammy said that Christmas was for giving. When my mom and dad were first married, they had very little, him being an E-2 and just coming out of basic and AIT training. Every year, for Christmas, Grammy gave mom some of her old ornaments. The hand-carved crosses and stars came from Grammy's father. The woolen angels with glittering wings came from her mother. The beautiful metal and glass ornaments, hand painted by craftsmen from all over the world, were treasures collected from all the locations where they had lived while in the military.

After she moved into the retirement village, she tried to give us the rest of them. "I don't need to keep these. I want to give them in the spirit in which they are meant." But we were full and had no more room on our tree or in our house. Mom suggested she decorate her own apartment. But Grammy insisted that she had all she needed to celebrate Christmas. So, she gave some to the home to decorate the big tree in the lobby and used the rest as gifts for nurses and other staff until all she had left was the one stocking.

At age fifteen, I thought Grammy's new house was cluttered with junk. No matter how much Mom begged her, Grammy insisted she stay in Williamsburg, Virginia. Mom wanted her to come closer to Virginia Beach, where we lived. But we dutifully made the trek out to visit her once a week. I begged out of visiting her many times, opting instead to spend my afternoon at the bookstore downtown.

After I graduated high school, I was accepted to attend William & Mary. Since the dorm was only fifteen minutes away from Grammy's home, I became the dutiful visitor. I'm not sure how long it took, but with each story Grammy told me about the items in her house, the junk slowly changed into meaningful memories. She told me glorious stories of trips to Amsterdam, London, and her ancestral home in Scottland. She reminisced about her childhood on the farm. She cried about the loss of Grandpa. All these little stories, bit by bit, turned her from just an old woman I needed to visit into my Grammy.

But the one story she wouldn't tell me was the one of the stocking. "Grammy, you have all these holidays in here, but where's Christmas?"

She pointed to the lonely, forlorn stocking and said, "Right there. And if you can't see it, then you're not old enough to know about it."

Over my next four years of college, I asked for clues. "Grammy, give me something to help figure it out, please?"

She would smile and shake her head. "You'll know, when you know."

I asked my mom and dad, but they hadn't any clue either. I asked friends that all speculated, "Maybe it's about life half full or half empty." Some said that perhaps it was a joke just to get people talking. Another theory was that it reminded Grammy of an event she didn't want to talk about.

Grammy's health slowly got worse. A year after I graduated, hospice took over her tiny apartment. On the many days before her death, I visited her, held her hand, read stories. I picked up items and retold the stories that she told me. When I gently removed the stocking and took it to her, hoping to get the story, she just smiled again and shook her head. "You'll understand soon. Promise me you'll keep it and hang it in your home."

I promised.

The next few days were tortuous as she slowly declined and finally made peace with the world. She died with a smile on her face, yet I agonized over it, thinking I should have done more. Had I done enough? Would she still be alive if I had done something different? Should I have started visiting her sooner? All the guilt played in my head.

After the funeral and the repast, the retirement home gave us a week to remove her belongings. Mom and Dad kept a few of the things that were important to them. Mom lifted the stocking off the wall and said, "Finally, we can get rid of this ugly thing."

"No, don't throw it away. I promised Grammy I'd keep it."

I took my box of knickknacks that I wanted to keep, and the stocking, back to my new apartment close to the building in which I now worked as an accountant. I carefully placed each memory in a position of honor on my shelves and tables, but some, including the stocking, stayed in a box which I shoved into the back of my closet.

A few years later, upon moving into a new home with my new husband Gary, I came across the long-forgotten box.

"What's that?" Gary asked.

"It's a box of stuff from my Grammy."

"Oh yeah, any treasures in there?"

"No, just memories and this." I held up the old stocking.

"What's that for? It looks like the mice got to it."

As I held up the stocking, I remembered the last days with Grammy when her body slowly shut down, her voice grew wispy, and her memories filled with holes, just like the stocking. But I was able to fill in the memories for her. I was able to keep her comfortable. I, with just my presence, gave her peace. That's when it hit me.

That worn-out old stocking was a reminder that even with all the beautiful photos, knickknacks, and other novelties from life, what you'll remember most is not the stuff you collected, but the time you spent with someone, the time you gave of yourself to make others feel better.

By sharing time with my Grammy, even when she was too worn out to continue, I was given the greatest gift of all. A family blessing of love and cherished memories.

I hung the stocking in a corner of the kitchen. Gary looked confused. "Why are you putting that there?"

"Because I wanted to be reminded of some things."

"What's that?"

"I can't tell you right now, but one day you'll know."

Though born in Pennsylvania and recently moved to Alabama, Sonja McGiboney calls herself a Virginian, having lived twenty-seven years between the cities of Newport News, Yorktown, and Smithfield. After graduating from West Virginia University, she married Dale and accompanied him on his twenty-five-year military career. She has two wonderful children, Rachel and Ryan, and a new grandson, Theo.

In writing her books, Sonja pulls from her life experience from moving with Dale and the Army. She has been a piano teacher, substitute teacher, primary teacher, file clerk, gas-station attendant, Family Readiness Group (FRG) Support assistant, FRG leader, mail clerk, credit reference associate, nanny, library assistant, photographer, and author.

In 2015, Sonja and Dale adopted a puppy and named her Jazzy. It was only natural that Sonja, a professional photographer, document Jazzy's antics. Jazzy's first photo album opened a path of creativity which generated 22 more Jazzy books, several non-Jazzy books, and a love of writing beyond children's pictures books.

Sonja's short stories are published in two anthologies, several online flash fiction sites, and her shortest story is published on https://101words.org. She is currently working on several fantasy novels for middle-grade students and a collection of short stories for adults.

You can find Sonja via her author website at https://sonjamcgiboney.wixsite.com/sonjamcgiboney

You can find Jazzy's books for ages 2 through 10 at: https://www.jazzysbooks.com/

Will and Trussy

by Jan Marry

As an anthropologist, he wasn't meant to have favorites, but he felt connected to Will. By the standards of the tribe, Will was a lone young male who came in and out of the place that they called the warehouse on a schedule that neither of them, nor anyone else, understood. The anthropologist looked down on the tribe as he studied them. He didn't gaze from on high because he felt superior—in fact, the tribe impressed him. But they insisted on moving about below him on the ground, a place so uncomfortable to him that looking down was his only choice. Afterward, the anthropologist claimed that he made contact with the tribe on purpose to further his studies. In reality, the trusses were slippery, and he was tired.

His anthropological notes were almost full. There was so much about the tribe that he needed to explain; he knew The Academy wouldn't believe him. The tribe acted civilized, even advanced, but they were blank to the fourth dimension, let alone dimensions five to seven. The anthropologist detected that, unbeknownst to the tribe, their warehouse work schedule used algorithms from the sixth dimension.

The tribe communicated in several ways. First, they opened a flap on their rounded upper appendage and produced sounds. Their preferred method was clutching a small metal and glass rectangle with two of their poor undeveloped limbs and pressing on its surface. They also swished about their upper limbs and pulled the muscles of their rounded upper appendage into circles and lines. The anthropologist detected that they were unaware of the information they conveyed with these body movements, but he saw it clearly as he observed from above.

The anthropologist studied hard and was soon able to interpret the meaning of the tribes' communications. The meaning was straightforward. A common exchange on the glass rectangles went, "LOL. I couldn't believe it!" with the recipient replying, "LMAO. You really told her!" The significance of the tribe's exchanges eluded the anthropologist; could civilized creatures spend so much time on utter inanities?

Inanities aside, the strength and adaptability of the tribe awed him. They casually moved their corporeal beings from conditions of high humidity and temperature to conditions that froze the precious water of their home. They even went unprotected under the cosmic rays that blasted for half of every cycle. His interpretations suggested that they sometimes enjoyed the cosmic rays when they made comments he knew he must have translated incorrectly. "It's a lovely day, isn't it? I'm so glad to see the sun."

Will, the lone male, came into the place during the dark part of the solar cycle. This was sensible to the anthropologist, but he knew that it wasn't the preference of most of the tribe. "Not night shift again!" they communicated. "I miss so much sleep."

The anthropologist was glad he'd found a sensible place to live. By the measurements of the tribe, the temperature was a steady sixty degrees Fahrenheit, the humidity a steady fifty percent. Electric tubes provided a stream of photons. The walls and roof were metal, held up by a system of braces that were perfect for him to use his fourteen tentacles to move around. He didn't need to risk the cosmic rays or wear a space suit. Members of the tribe came in and out of this place so he could observe them.

Every time Will arrived at the warehouse, the

anthropologist's heart lifted. He knew this was impossible because he didn't have a heart and lifting implied a structure to dimensionality of up and down, but the anthropologist *knew* his life was better when Will was present.

The anthropologist suspected that Will had detected him. The photon-emitting tubes confused the anthropologist, but in the dimension of the tribe, they enabled their most important sense: sight. Will looked up. "Hello, you lovely tentacled thing," he said. He rubbed his chin. "What are you? Where are you from?"

For a time after this, (the anthropologist wasn't sure how long, he measured time differently to the tribe), the anthropologist felt eager anticipation for Will to come into the warehouse and look up. Will made comments that the anthropologist had to admit were true, even if they reflected badly on an inter-stellar adventurer. "Wherever you've come from, it looks like you like it here in this warehouse. And you're the only one. It must be very lonely being the only one." Will blinked his eyes, which had become shiny. "I thought it was lonely for me, but there are plenty of people here."

The instructions were very clear for the anthropologist. He was required to observe, record his notes, and leave. Contact was forbidden. Strictly speaking, he was also meant to travel all over the planet, even if he had to wear his space suit, but the anthropologist chose to ignore that.

The anthropologist declared to himself that Will

was an important case study, so he had an obligation to science to stay in the warehouse. Will communicated with his flapping upper appendage less than some of the other tribe members. He barely used his glass rectangle. The anthropologist learned that when the members of the tribe spent hours moving boxes and bits and pieces from here to there in the warehouse, it was called a "job." They communicated about it a lot. "I hate this job," or "I'm looking for a new job."

Will was assigned a forked machine for his job. The anthropologist tried communicating with the machine that the tribe called a forklift, but it didn't communicate back. The movement and warmth that the anthropologist knew gave life to cold metal objects barely animated the machine. Its internal combustion engine was amazingly primitive and its mind so sluggish that the anthropologist found he could not connect with its life force. The anthropologist noted that Will possessed the ability to communicate with his forked machine, which showed him to be an advanced life form. As he propelled the machine, Will opened the flap on his face and communicated. "Gently does it. Don't swing too far! That was close."

Periodically the tribe members gathered for what they called a break and Will displayed approval of the other's communication by lifting the corners of his face flap, although he rarely made sounds in return. Many of the tribe tried to avoid doing their assigned jobs of moving bits and bobs around the warehouse, and in and out of the terrifying doors into the cosmic rays. They stood in corners and communicated, and despite his advanced training in the fifth dimension, the anthropologist couldn't work out what they meant. "Did you see that play just before half time?" and, "I can't believe that the ref let that one go." Sometimes they gathered in clusters in the cosmic rays and inhaled exudates from a small burning stick. The exudates were very harmful to their health, so the anthropologist wasn't sure why they did it. For the entire time he was scheduled, Will propelled his assigned machine here and there in the warehouse. The anthropologist admired this. He had been brought up that working to the best of your ability was highly valued.

The warehouse became busier. More members of the tribe were scheduled for each shift. Their communications changed. "Did you hear about the holiday bonuses this year?" said one, with an expression showing relief from the stress that the word *debt* caused in him.

"I'm saving up to buy that new doll thing that all the kids want. I don't want my daughter to miss out," said another, whose face softened every time he said the words *my daughter.*

"Are you going to the tree lighting in Williamsburg?" a female of middle years said to Will. "You should come. I love to sing carols in the middle of those old buildings."

Will muttered something unintelligible back but the

anthropologist detected Will's feeling that celebratory displays at this time of year were for other people.

"What are you doing for Thanksgiving and Christmas?" became a common refrain.

Will listened but didn't say much in return. The anthropologist could feel the emotions that talking about Christmas brought out in the tribe members. Most felt happy and optimistic, mixed with stress. Some tribe members like Will felt sad.

The day of the Connection, the anthropologist detected from the beginning of Will's shift that Will wasn't properly balanced. He squinted at the photon-emitters and communicated to another tribe member, the female of middle years who had asked him about the tree lighting, "I think I'm getting a migraine. I hope I get through the whole shift."

"Honey, I hope you feel better. Don't stay if it gets too bad. It ain't safe." The female of middle years made sure she saved him homemade cookies when she brought them into the warehouse. She had a soft expression on her face. The anthropologist saw this expression when the tribe talked about their offspring, spouses, and people with whom they developed friendships. When they were interested in mating with another person, their expression resembled the face that indicated that they needed sustenance.

On the night of the migraine, Will's task was to take

boxes of food from one location to another on the forklift. He learned where to put them because a distant electronic voice sent instructions into a headset covering his ears.

The anthropologist slipped from truss to truss above Will. He sensed that Will wanted to stop concentrating and shut his eyes. The forklift wove from side to side along the aisle, rather than trundling in Will's usual satisfyingly straight line.

As he observed, the anthropologist's suckers wound and unwound around the metal roof truss. He reminded himself sternly that his task was to observe and not interfere.

Will's forklift bumped into a shelf. Boxes and bits wobbled but didn't fall.

The anthropologist moved down the trusses, closer to Will.

Will took off his headset and hooked it over the back of his seat. He got the fork stuck under a shelf. He let go of the controls and massaged his head with his hands. He grabbed the controls and backed up. The forks screeched on the metal shelf, and he shook his head as if to shake the sound out of his ears.

Will put his headset back on and trundled too fast along the aisles. He squinted at the numbers on the ends of the shelves, then headed down the far aisle. Above, the anthropologist hurried after him.

Halfway down the farthest aisle, Will took a deep

breath and pushed a lever back. He shut his eyes. The box rose toward the high shelf where it belonged. The forklift began to tilt but with closed eyes, Will didn't notice. Two wheels rose off the concrete floor.

Before he could think, the anthropologist scrambled down. He gripped the shelves with four or five of his tentacles while he reached out quickly and grabbed the forklift with several more. The forklift settled back on four wheels with a slight jolt.

Will opened his eyes and looked into the face of the anthropologist. "Hello, Trussy. I knew you were there."

"Greetings to William John," the anthropologist communicated. His own tribe rarely communicated directly to any individual, but this felt right.

Will turned his face flap up at the corners. "Thank you for saving me." He rubbed his head again. "Don't worry, I won't tell anyone you're here."

They stared at each other for several moments longer, then Will said, "I'd better get back to work. The sooner I'm finished, the sooner I can go home and sleep."

"Sleep and heal, William James," the anthropologist communicated. "I will continue to enjoy your company after more cosmic radiation cycles have passed."

"Yes, I'll sleep this off," said Will. He laughed. "In fact, I think seeing you has made my headache go away." He lifted the corners of the flap on his upper appendage higher than the anthropologist had ever seen, and the anthropologist knew he was happy.

The anthropologist liked the word *Trussy* that Will had uttered. It had a soft, sibilant slide. His own language didn't have words and certainly didn't have anything resembling names.

Trussy, as he liked to think of himself now, heard from The Academy. They had received his reports about the tribe and, as Trussy had suspected, they didn't believe him. They wanted Trussy to complete his field studies in this part of the galaxy and return to where he had come from. Trussy didn't think of it as *home*. That wasn't a word that his tribe used. When Trussy thought about it, he realized that not only was *home* not a word, but it also wasn't a concept for his tribe. Trussy liked the concept of home. He especially liked the idea of this warehouse being his home. He wanted his home to be where Will came in regularly.

Will and the warehouse workers called other places home. They talked about their homes a lot, but not always with the joy that Trussy felt about his new home. "My landlord hasn't fixed that leak yet. He said he would. And that's *after* the rent went up."

They complained about traveling to work. Trussy didn't understand why they didn't use the seventh dimension to project their corporeal bodies to the place they needed to be. "I am going to be completely bald from pulling my own hair out if they don't finish the construction on I-64 soon," was a common, but inexplicable refrain.

As Trussy felt something inside himself softening in the way of the tribe when they talked about their offspring, he found that he detected their negative emotions more easily and fully.

"I can't believe this schedule! I asked for Christmas Eve off." It was the female of middle years who was kind to Will. They were looking at papers pinned to a noticeboard outside the break room. Her warm, rusty orange emotions were spiked with reaching shadows.

Will showed that he sensed her emotions as well. "What's wrong?" he asked.

She shook her head. "My husband's in the army. Christmas Eve is the only time we'll get to be together. The kids have such crazy schedules, what with the stepparents and some at college and everything."

"Can't you meet another day?"

Her eyes glinted in the way Trussy had seen before. "No. It won't work. And the little ones *care* who they celebrate with for Christmas."

Will cleared his throat. "I'll do the Christmas Eve shift."

She turned to look at him. "Are you sure?"

"It's okay." Will swallowed. "I don't have anyone special to be with anyway."

Trussy saw that Will was sad about Christmas Eve and that he wanted to return the kindness of the female.

"Thank you. Thank you. I'll ask to swap." She gestured wide with both arms as if to hug Will, then she saw the expression on his face. She laughed. "I'll just pat your arm. But you're a kind boy, Will."

On Christmas Eve, steady rain poured down. It filled gutters and drains and dragged down the spirits of the few people of the tribe who came to the warehouse. "They said we could make this a short shift if we get everything done," one said to Will.

Will looked at the piles of boxes. "I think there's plenty to do."

"I think those boxes will wait. I'm going home early."

Will worked hard as usual, but he kept looking at the time piece on his wrist for reasons that Trussy didn't understand. He stopped his forklift in the middle of an aisle and abruptly turned it off. Trussy hurried over in case Will's head pain meant he couldn't concentrate again in a dangerous way.

Will looked at Trussy. "I can feel you're worried." He laughed. "Don't worry." He jumped down off the forklift. "I was waiting for midnight. At midnight on Christmas Eve, it becomes Christmas. Come over here. I have something for you."

In a corner, Will had covered a large box with a plastic tablecloth decorated with pine trees and laughing bearded men in red and white. He had set out two sets of refreshments. In a crude way, the sugar-butter squares resembled the decorations on the tablecloth. "I decorated the cookies myself." Will looked shy. "I'm not very good at it. They turned out a bit wonky."

Trussy communicated reassurance into Will's mind.

Will smiled and lifted a paper cup of juice. "Cheers, Trussy."

Trussy lifted the other paper cup of juice with two of his fourteen tentacles. He could communicate directly into Will's mind, but this occasion called for something more. He gathered his thoughts to make waves in the air in the method the tribe called sound. To his own senses it didn't quite come out the way the tribe communicated with each other. He croaked, "Merry Christmas, Will."

Will lifted his paper cup. "Merry Christmas to you, Trussy. I'm glad you've come to stay with us here."

About the Author

Jan Marry has published short stories, personal essays, articles, and book reviews in several outlets including *Nature Futures, The Hopkins Review, Virginia Libraries* and *Library Journal.* Her first novel, *Sweet Tea and Anzac Biscuits,* is being released soon by Blue Fortune Enterprises, LLC. She is a member of the Chesapeake Bay Writers and the James River Writers. Jan has an MA in science writing from Johns Hopkins and a Master of Library Science from the University of Illinois, a BA in English from the University of Maryland, and a BSc in zoology from the University of Otago.

Jan has been a librarian for two decades and revels in book groups, book displays, writing book reviews, and sharing books through library programs. In 2021, she was awarded the Donna G. Cote Virginia Librarian of the Year. Originally from New Zealand, Jan lived in six countries with her miliary family before settling on a small farm in southeast Virginia where herding chickens and cats at the same time is a frequent (and non-metaphorical) occurrence. You can contact Jan at janmarrywriter@gmail.com and learn more about her work at https://janmarry.wordpress.com/

Thank you for reading this collection of holiday stories!

For more information on Chesapeake Bay Writers, visit
https://www.chesapeakebaywriters.org/
For more information about Blue Fortune Enterprises,
LLC, visit https://blue-fortune.com/

*May you hold the spirit of goodwill within your heart all the
year long and share it throughout your world.*
Narielle Living

9 781961 548169